CO...

'Take the medal in to ...
what it's worth at lea...
you'll have to give it in ... ...ly worth a couple
of pounds, it won't really matter, will it?'

'Yes, it will,' said Lisa slowly. She knew just what
they would all think, but she had to say it anyway. 'It
might have – sentimental value. It might belong to a
war widow, or an old soldier. Someone might be terribly upset about losing it. I think you should hand it
in to the police.'

'You would,' said Sally-Anne spitefully. 'Typical copper's kid. I suppose you think we should just take it to
your dad right now. Or are *you* going to tell him, if we
don't?'

For Naomi and Sophie

COPPER'S KID

Yvonne Coppard

RED FOX

Published by Arrow Books Limited
20 Vauxhall Bridge Road, London SW1V 2SA
An imprint of the Random Century Group
London Melbourne Sydney Auckland
Johannesburg and agencies throughout the world
First published in 1989 by Hutchinson Children's Books
Red Fox edition 1990
Copyright © Yvonne Coppard Quirk 1989

Set in Sabon by Input Typesetting Ltd
Made and printed in Great Britain
by Courier International Ltd
Tiptree, Essex

ISBN 0 09 963880 0

One

As soon as she saw the little white car turn into Elderberry Walk, Lisa dodged back from the landing. She ran across the hall to the back bedroom. A whistle had been put ready by the open window. Lisa picked it up and gave three short blasts. Her job was done now, and she leaned her elbows on the sill to watch.

Over in the far left-hand corner of the garden, where the Tennesons' wall met Old Fusspot Fogarty's fence, Lisa saw a movement. The tree on Old Fogarty's side swayed. Then a sack appeared, pushed by unseen hands. It fell heavily into the honeysuckle. Lisa grinned with satisfaction. The sack looked quite full.

The scrunching of gravel as Old Fogarty pulled into his drive sent a nervous shiver through Lisa's stomach. She watched more closely. Where on earth were they?

A hand came into view at the top of the fence, followed by a headful of shaggy dark hair. Then the rest of Zeke appeared, hauling himself over the fence and landing with a crash in the honeysuckle. He stood up and waved at Lisa. She made a sign to him, drawing her hand across her throat to tell him to be quick. They both heard the screech of the garage door being pulled up. Lisa hoped the others would realize that, on a hot summer day like this, sound carried easily. She could hear Sally-Anne giggling, even from here. What if Old

5

Fusspot Fogarty or his wife got suspicious, and decided to come round to the back of the house?

Sally-Anne was the next to arrive on the top of the fence. Being almost two years younger than the rest of the Gang, she needed help over the fence. Zeke took her hands and she jumped down. Considering how podgy she was, thought Lisa, she landed surprisingly lightly on her feet.

Fliss came over with smooth, swift movements that showed her training – she had already won several medals for gymnastics. She looked up to the window and waved as Zeke picked up the sack and moved off across the lawn. Then Fliss beckoned to Lisa, pointing to the row of cypress trees on the other side of the garden. Behind these lay the Gang Headquarters. Lisa nodded, waved back, and shut the window.

'What are *you* up to, young lady?'

The voice behind her almost made Lisa jump out of her skin. She whirled round. Fliss and Zeke's dad was in the doorway, laughing at her.

'You look very guilty, Lisa. Are you planning to steal the family silver? Or is it your turn to be on the lookout for yet another raid on poor old Fogarty?'

'What? Of course not, Mr Tenneson. No!' said Lisa at once, guilt making her voice over-shrill. 'I . . . er . . . Fliss just asked me to get something for her – her hairbrush!' she finished desperately. Lisa grabbed a hairbrush from the dressing table, and dodged past Mr Tenneson into the hallway.

'Well, I'm very happy to know Felicity is beginning to take an interest in her appearance at last,' grinned Mr Tenneson. He walked past her, tweaking one of her blonde bunches. 'You've got a ribbon missing again,' he said over his shoulder as he went into his study at the end of the hallway.

Lisa knew she was blushing because her face felt so hot. She ran down the stairs, through the dining room and out into the garden.

The Tennesons and the Fogartys had the two largest houses in Elderberry Walk. They stood right at the end of the cul-de-sac, so they had half of the broad sweep of the close each, with garden on all four sides. The houses stood at the top of a hill, as well as right at the end. So if you stood at an upstairs window, you could see exactly what was going on in the whole of Elderberry Walk. That was what made the Tennesons' landing such a good lookout spot.

Lisa liked the job of lookout. It was not quite as exciting as leading the raid, or as risky, but it was important to do it properly.

As she rounded the cypress trees, Lisa called out, 'Peter Pan's Pudding!' which had been Zeke's choice of password for today, and the door of the hut opened. Looking round cautiously, though no one could possibly see her, Lisa slipped in.

Fliss knelt on the floor with the sack in front of her. The apples spilled out, glowing yellow-red in the dim, dusty light of the hut. Pushing her dark curls impatiently back over her shoulder so that they became an ever-more tangled mess, Fliss was sorting out the apples into five piles.

'I'll say this for Old Fogarty,' she said. 'He's got lovely apples – I wish we had trees like that.'

'He doesn't look after them, either,' said Zeke. 'I don't think he even *likes* apples – he's just too mean to offer them to us. He leaves them rotting on the ground.

He's too busy being nosy and making a nuisance of himself to pick them, I suppose.'

'We're doing him a favour, then, aren't we?' laughed Fliss. She took an apple and tossed it into the air, rubbing it on her sleeve before taking a bite. 'We're saving him a lot of work. He ought to be thankful.'

They all laughed, and Lisa flopped down on the pile of cushions to watch Fliss share out. Zeke, who was going to be in the Third Year of Lee Moor High School when they went back after the holidays, was leader of the Gang. He was given two extra apples as a sign of the extra responsibility. A half-share was set aside for Gary. His mum had sent him to the shops at the last moment, so he had to back out of the raid. Zeke had decided that, since it was not his fault, it was only fair that he should have some of the spoils.

Lisa leaned back on her cushions contentedly, munching one of her apples. The garden hut, their Headquarters, was one of her favourite places. It had been a Christmas present to Fliss and Zeke. It was typical of Mr and Mrs Tenneson to come up with an unusual idea like that. Lisa was a bit shy of them, especially Mr Tenneson because he was a well-known writer, and even came on the television sometimes. But she bet they were great to have as parents. They let Fliss and Zeke do almost whatever they wanted to, not like her own mum and dad who were always telling her what to do.

The hut was their own private place, and even had a proper lock and key, which Zeke always kept with him. Inside, the Gang had made it look really cosy, begging whatever they could for furniture. An old kitchen table stood in the corner, and a bathroom stool. Each member of the Gang had their own pile of cushions and a saucepan or jug for their own particular treasures.

8

There were two shelves on the wall holding magazines, a sweet jar with biscuits in it, and a half-full bottle of lemonade. Above these hung a lantern, another present to Fliss and Zeke. It looked just like an oil lamp, but it was battery operated and quite safe to use in the hut. The circular rug on the floor was the one which Lisa's mum had given them when she redecorated the living room. There was even a rickety camp bed – sometimes Zeke slept out here. Lisa did not much like the idea of that herself. It was awfully dark and quiet in this part of the garden.

'Lisa, Lisa, are you there?' Fliss was waving her hand in front of Lisa's eyes.

'Sorry. I was just thinking how nice it is in here. We've made it look really good.'

'*You* didn't have much to do with it,' put in Sally-Anne. 'You were on holiday when we did most of it.' Her eyes gleamed maliciously, looking small and piggy-like behind the round glasses.

'Shut up, Sal,' said Fliss mildly. 'Here, Lisa – what are you doing with my hairbrush?'

'Oh, I forgot. Your dad caught me looking out of the window. He asked me if we were raiding the Fogartys' again, as if he knew exactly what we were doing! I told him you wanted your hairbrush, but I don't think he believed me.'

Zeke snorted. 'Of course he didn't. Does Fliss look like the sort of girl who suddenly decides to brush her hair in the middle of the morning?'

Lisa looked across at a grinning Fliss, and had to agree it was not very likely. Fliss was very pretty, at least Lisa had always thought so. She would swap her own pale, straight hair and blue eyes any day for those dark curls and deep brown eyes. Fliss, however, did not care about looks at all, and had no time for unimportant details like clean faces or tidy hair. There was a smudge of soil on her nose at the moment, covering her freckles. Twigs and leaves were still caught in the hair which tumbled down her back. Fliss pushed her fingers through her hair impatiently.

'It doesn't matter – he won't tell.'

'He does know, then?' said Lisa, astonished.

Fliss shrugged. 'Suspects, at least – probably knows. Not a lot passes Dad. He *seems* to be very wrapped up in his books and TV scripts and things, but even when he's working he's got half an ear tuned to whatever is going on around the place. He says it gives him new ideas for stories and things.'

'My dad would hit the roof if he found out we had gone scrumping in Old Fogarty's garden,' said Lisa enviously.

'Of course he would,' said Sally-Anne. 'He's a cop, isn't he? A Policeman Plod. Stands to reason he's a goody-goody.'

Lisa flushed angrily. 'He's a detective inspector, actually. And keeping the law doesn't make him a goody-goody, either, not in the way you mean. You'd be the first to whine and complain if there were no police around to protect you. I'm sick of the way you keep going on . . .'

'Ooh, touchy, aren't we? said Sally-Anne. But she kept quiet after an angry look from Zeke, and started sulkily on her second apple.

'Take no notice of Sal,' said Zeke kindly. 'We know your dad is all right. What would he do, though? If he knew?'

'He wouldn't like it,' admitted Lisa. 'Or my mum. But you should hear them talk about what they got up

10

to when they were kids.' She pointed to the pile of apples. 'This is nothing, compared to what they did.'

Fliss had finished counting. There were two apples left over. These were put with the biscuits for emergencies. For a while there was a contented silence, with only the steady munch of apples and the flick of pages turning.

Footsteps approaching the hut had them all alert at once. 'Peter Pan's Pudding,' came a loud whisper. Lisa jumped up to answer the door.

'Gary! You took your time. It's all over now.'

'Ah, well.' Gary stood, grinning at his friends. Like Fliss and Lisa, he would be moving up into the Second Year at Lee Moor High in September, but it was difficult to believe he was not still in the Juniors, like Sally-Anne. He was not any taller than her, and much thinner. Lisa, who knew what went on in his house but was sworn to secrecy, believed that his uncle did not let him have enough to eat.

The first time she had actually seen bruises on Gary, she had been shocked. He had rolled his sleeves up, unthinkingly, at the beach, when they were hunting for crabs. There was a line of four small bruises and a slightly larger one. Gary had caught her gaze, and quickly rolled his sleeve down again. But Lisa knew that pattern of bruises from a book she had taken down from her mum's shelf one day.

'Was that your uncle?' she had asked, trying to sound casual, the way Mum did when she was dealing with real trouble. And Gary had told her. It was only when his uncle was really angry – or drunk – and usually it was only a clout round the ear, or a hard grip like the one which had caused the bruises on his arm. But sometimes . . . Lisa, the daughter not only of a policeman but of a social worker, did not need the details. She remembered the other times, when she and the Gang had wondered about Gary: the heat wave last summer, when he had worn school shirts with long sleeves, instead of the scraggy vests which everyone else wore; the days he had refused to go into the sea with them, watching from the shore, fully dressed except for his shoes and socks. And it had all fallen into place. She had understood, too, why Gary's mother, on the rare occasions she was seen in public, looked so worried – frightened, even. She had wanted to ask, but then Gary would never have talked to her about it, and she had sensed he needed to talk.

Lisa had tried to persuade Gary to tell someone, but in the end had promised to keep quiet. They shared the secret together, and it made them the closest friends of all the Gang. Zeke and Fliss, she knew, found this a little hard to understand – they liked Gary, but considered him to be rather 'moody', as Fliss put it. Lisa wished she could explain why he seemed that way. But Gary trusted her, and though she would have given anything not to have to keep such a secret to herself, Lisa was proud of being trusted and special.

Now, as he stood looking at them all, Gary did not look as pale as usual. His thin face, under the short brown hair, was a bit flushed, and his eyes were somehow smiling just as much as his mouth.

'Gary, my boy, you're up to something,' said Lisa at once. 'What have you been doing?'

Two

'He does look like a boy with something to hide, doesn't he?' laughed Fliss. 'Come on then, Gary. Tell all.'

'Can you keep a secret?' Gary's eyes briefly met Lisa's and she looked away. Gary put his hand in his pocket and closed his first around something.

'Oh, no. We're bound to blab,' said Zeke. 'We'll tell everyone. We'll take a whole page ad. in the *Daily Mirror*: "Gary's Dreadful Secret Revealed – By Best Friends". We'll –'

'All right, all right. Just look at this.' Gary held out his hand and the Gang gathered round to look.

It was a round silver medallion, like a coin, resting snugly in the palm of Gary's hand. On one side was the head of a youngish lady in a tiara, and the words 'Victoria Regina'.

'Who's she?' asked Sally-Anne.

'Queen Victoria,' said Zeke; 'you know.' He stuck his nose in the air and said in a shrill voice, ' "We are not amused." '

On the other side was another woman, 'Britannia, I think,' said Zeke, and she was sitting on the back of a horse – a sort of horse anyway. It had a huge fish tail where legs should have been.

Attached to the coin was a dark, stripey ribbon with little bars stuck on it. They had place names on them: 'Algeria', 'Egypt', and 'Trafalgar'.

'A brooch?' said Sally-Anne. 'What do you want a brooch for?'

'It's a medal, stupid,' said Lisa, glad of the chance to get back at Sally-Anne for being rotten about Dad.

Sally-Anne flushed. 'That's what I meant. What are you doing with it?'

'I found it,' said Gary triumphantly. 'In the alley.'

'The alley?' they chorused.

'What was it doing there?' asked Sally-Anne.

Gary shrugged. 'I don't know. It was lying in the alley, sort of under a cigarette packet someone had dropped. I trod on it when I was climbing the wall.'

The Tennesons' garden wall ran along the alley for most of its length. The alley started at Elderberry Walk, right next to the Tennesons' front gates. At the end of their garden the alley turned sharp right towards Wood Lane, while the Tennesons' back wall went to the left, backing on to the school field. The Gang often came down the alley from Wood Lane and nipped over the garden wall. It was right next to the hut, and because of the cypress trees no one from the house could see them coming and going.

'Someone must have dropped it, I suppose,' said Fliss. 'But who on earth would be carrying an old war medal around?'

'What are you going to do with it, Gary?' asked Zeke. 'I mean are you going to give it to the police, or just ask around?'

'Or keep it,' added Sally-Anne. 'You might even be able to sell it – there's a shop in Plymouth that sells that sort of stuff. I've been there with my dad.' Plymouth was the nearest town, about four miles away.

'I might at that,' said Gary. 'After all, no one could

have cared much about it. We would have noticed someone searching.'

Lisa thought this was not a very good argument, but she waited for Fliss or Zeke to say so. They looked a bit uncomfortable, but neither of them spoke.

'Take it in to Plymouth,' said Sally-Anne. 'See what it's worth, at least. If it's really valuable, well, you'll have to give it in. But if it's only a couple of pounds, it won't really matter, will it?'

'Yes, it will,' said Lisa slowly. She knew just what they would all think, but she had to say it anyway. 'It might have – sentimental value. It might belong to a war widow, or an old soldier. Someone might be terribly upset about losing it. I think you should hand it in to the police.'

'You would,' said Sally-Anne spitefully. 'Typical copper's kid. I suppose you think we should just take it to your dad right now. Or are *you* going to tell him, if we don't?'

Lisa felt her face going hot again as anger and misery churned up together inside her. She had known Sally-Anne would say something like that.

'No,' she said, as coldly as she could manage. 'My dad's far too important to be bothered with lost property, and he works in Plymouth, anyway. The constable at the desk in the local station would deal with this. But it's Gary's find, not ours. It's for him to decide, not me – but not you, either.'

The two girls glowered at each other.

'What are you going to do, Gary?' asked Fliss quietly.

Gary weighed the medal in his hand, considering. 'If it's Victorian, the bloke who won it won't be alive any more, will he? Or his widow. So I don't think it can have much sentimental value, Lisa. I think . . . I think

15

I'm going to try and sell it,' he said finally. 'Like Sal says, if it's really valuable, I'll hand it in at once. I'll go this afternoon, straight after lunch. Who's coming with me?'

'Not me,' said Zeke quickly. 'Or Fliss. Mum's taking us to an art exhibition this afternoon – they're showing one of her engravings.'

Their mother was an artist. She made peculiar pictures, full of sharp lines and impossible colours. No one in the Gang could understand them at all, but of course no one would dream of saying so aloud.

Sally-Anne gave an exaggerated sigh. 'S'pose it'll have to be me, then, Gary. Because Lisa won't, will she? Far too risky for *her* . . . .'

'I'll go, if you want me to,' said Lisa, stung.

Gary's face brightened. 'Thanks, Lisa. You can stay here, Sal. I don't suppose your mum would let you go into Plymouth, anyway.'

'No,' said Lisa. 'You're only just ten, aren't you? It's a bit young yet. Never mind.' She tried not to smile. It was her point this time.

'If I get a bit of money,' said Gary dreamily, 'we'll have a celebration. And I'll buy Mum a present – or just not ask for pocket money for a while. Then *he* won't have a chance to moan on about how much it costs to keep me.'

The Gang shifted uncomfortably. They all knew that when Gary's father had died his uncle had only agreed to give them a home because Social Services had made him feel guilty about leaving his brother's widow in the lurch. He made no secret of the fact that he didn't want either of them around, although only Lisa knew how far he went in his bitterness against them, behind the closed doors of his neat semi-detached in Elderberry

16

Walk. Gary's mother was always unhappy, and didn't seem to be able to face anything outside the front door. But the rest of the Gang came from safe, secure homes. They moaned about their parents to each other, of course, but each one secretly felt very thankful that they were not in Gary's shoes.

Lisa did not believe that what Gary was doing was right, but she could understand how he felt, and she realized how awful it must be to be so helpless, so dependent on a brutal man; like being in a prison with a cruel jailor, and no hope of escape. The realization that probably there were lots more families living like this made her feel sad, and old, like a grown-up. She hoped the sad and grown-up parts did not always go together like this.

'Never mind, Gary,' said Lisa, putting a tentative hand on his arm. 'You've been on the waiting list ages – a council house has to come up soon. Then you and your mum can leave the old misery to get on with it.'

Gary gave a thin smile and turned away. The others stood about uselessly, wishing there was something they could do and knowing there was nothing. Gary was proud, and hated anyone feeling sorry for him – Lisa was the only one who could express sympathy without being embarrassed.

Sally-Anne was still glowering at Lisa. She had wanted to be the one to go with Gary; she was fed up with being the youngest. Sally-Anne would simply have gone, without telling her mum.

Gary and Lisa arranged to meet at the alleyway after lunch. The bus left from Wood Lane at ten past one. That would give them plenty of time to go to the shop and be back by four thirty, when Lisa's mum would be

17

home. The Gang went their separate ways, promising to meet back at the hut at five thirty.

Lisa only lived four doors away from the Tennesons, and she let herself in the through the back door. She could hear her brother's stereo, as usual, when she was halfway up the drive. As Lisa climbed the stairs to his room, she could feel the vibrations of the bass, beneath her feet.

'Chris!' She knocked on his door. 'Chris!' He could not hear her. Lisa just walked in.

The stuffiness was almost unbearable – it was blazing hot outside, but complaints from the neighbours made Chris keep the windows closed whenever he was playing the stereo, which was most of the time. Chris sat on the bed, with his electric guitar trailing its lead. It was not plugged in, but he was pretending to play along with the group. It was some time before he saw Lisa. When he did, he did not look at all embarrassed. He raised his eyebrows in a sort of enquiry, and then turned back to his guitar. Finally, Lisa went and stood right in front of him.

'Chris,' she mouthed. 'It's lunchtime.'

'What?' he shouted above the music, with an expression of annoyance.

'LUNCHTIME!' bellowed Lisa.

Reluctantly, Chris turned down the volume. Mum and Dad paid Chris, who was seventeen and studying for 'A' levels, to look after Lisa on the days when they were both at work. She was blowed if she was going to get her own lunch. No one paid *her* for looking after herself, even though this is precisely what she did, many times, when Chris was left in charge. He didn't even always walk home with her from school when he was

18

supposed to, and in the holidays he took virtually no notice of her at all.

'I want my lunch,' said Lisa. 'I've got to go out soon.'

'Where are you going?' said Chris, still picking at his guitar. 'Mum will want you home, when she gets back.'

'Only to Plymouth – with Gary,' she added quickly, because she knew she would not be allowed on her own.

Chris raised his eyebrows again. 'Oh, a date is it? That's lovely. Your very first boyfriend, eh, Lisa? Ah!'

Lisa threw a pillow at him. 'Shut up, Chris. I want my lunch. You're supposed to get it all ready. If I've got to get my own, then I want some of the money Mum will give you.'

Chris ruffled her hair as he got up from the bed, dislodging the remaining ribbon from her bunches.

'Nice try, Sis, but tough luck. I, being incredibly well-organized, prepared lunch ages ago – it's on top of the fridge.'

Lisa went downstairs, disappointed. She had been hoping to wangle a bit of money; she only had just enough for the bus fare. But Chris had indeed got lunch ready. A peanut butter sandwich, wrapped in clingfilm, a bag of crisps and an apple stood beside a glass of juice on the fridge. There was also a small chocolate bar. Chris must have bought that himself.

'Thanks, Chris!' she yelled up the stairs, but the music had begun again and he could not hear her.

Lisa loaded her lunch onto a tray and sat down on the floor in front of the television. It was difficult to hear what was being said, and it was a programme for very young children, anyway. Lisa watched the presenters prancing around, pretending to be horses, then cats and finally – she thought – cows.

'They must feel like right idiots,' she thought. It had never occurred to her before, but the more she thought about this the funnier it seemed. In the end she developed a fit of the giggles so strong she almost choked on her sandwich.

Even so, she could not quite push Gary's determination to sell the medal out of her mind. Lisa wished she had not been daft enough to say she would go with him. It was Sally-Anne's fault. That smug smile when she thought Lisa would say no had been very annoying. Well, she had wiped the smile off Sally-Anne's face, all right. But was it worth it?

'I just hope no one cares about the medal,' she thought unhappily, 'or that it turns out to be worthless anyway.'

What if the shopkeeper got suspicious and thought they'd stolen the medal? What if they were both arrested and taken to the police station? Dad would be called in; he was on duty this afternoon. 'Sorry to bother you, Sir. We've got this young girl downstairs caught handling stolen property. Seems she's your daughter, Sir . . . .' Lisa went hot at the thought. He would never forgive her.

For a moment, she toyed with the idea of pretending to feel ill, and not going at all. Then she imagined Sally-Anne's fat smile of triumph, and what she would say to the others, behind Lisa's back.

Miserably, Lisa counted out her bus fare to check again that she had enough. She put her plate and glass by the sink, for Chris to wash up.

There was nothing else for it. She would have to go.

Three

Gary knew where the shop was, and led Lisa quickly through the stream of people crowding the main shopping areas. Plymouth was always very busy in the summer. Mum and Dad found the tourists annoying, and complained about the traffic, and having to fight for space in the car parks. Lisa got a bit fed up herself with the crowded beaches and the long queues for everything, but on the whole she rather liked the colour and noise the tourists brought with them. Today she was particularly grateful for it. Two children wandering around town were not worth noticing, with so much going on.

They turned off Armada Way, which was one of the big main streets, onto a quieter road at the edge of town. The shops here were not 'shopping' shops. There was an estate agent, an 'Instant Print' shop, a dental surgery and a big antique shop. Next to the antique shop, looking very small and squalid, stood 'Maxwell's Military'.

'Military what?' asked Lisa.

'Military everything, I'd say.' Gary nodded at the window display.

It was not very artistic; it looked a bit like the bric-a-brac stall at the annual school fete. There were compasses, old maps, ornamental daggers, buckles, boxes of stamps, and a pile of old books. At the back of the window were several black trays with medals pinned onto them. A handwritten sign said, 'Military Memorabilia Bought and Sold – Good Prices'.

Lisa peered through the glass. Inside the shop she could make out a suit of armour, lots of swords and old-fashioned pistols hanging on the walls, and lines of shelves. An old man in a brown overall sat at the counter, reading a newspaper. Lisa turned her attention to the medals. She and Gary scanned them carefully.

'I can't see one that looks the same, can you?' she said.

'No. That could be good, though. It might mean he'll want this one more.'

'What are we going to say?' Lisa's heart was pounding, and she felt hot and giddy. It was ridiculous; she had done nothing wrong. So why did she feel so . . . ? 'Guilty', she told herself. 'Guilty is what you feel. Because you know you should try and stop Gary from doing this.' But Lisa knew, too, that she was not going to stop him.

Gary shrugged. 'I'll think of something. You can stay here, if you like. In fact,' he added kindly, 'it would be better – two of us might make him more suspicious.' Gary knew Lisa too well for her to bother to look regretful, and he smiled when he saw the look of relief on her face. He took a deep breath. 'Well, here goes.'

'Good luck,' whispered Lisa, and she squeezed his arm. She watched Gary walk into the shop, quite breezily, hands in pockets. When the old man looked up, she moved quickly away from the window and went to look in the antique shop.

Gary seemed to be gone an awfully long time. Perhaps the old man had called the police? Lisa moved further down the street, and studied the photographs of houses in the estate agent's window. She would wait five more minutes and then make herself scarce. Lisa knew a lot of the constables at Plymouth Police Station, and she did not want to risk being seen when they came to get Gary. Of course she felt bad leaving him, but there was nothing she could do to help. She would go home and . . . Lisa realized, with horror, that she had no ticket. They had bought returns and she had given hers to Gary, because there was a hole in her pocket. She had no money, either. She would have to walk home, and even if she could remember the way, she would never be home by the time Mum came in from work.

At that moment of blind panic, a hand gripped her elbow.

'Come on. Let's get out of here!'

Lisa let out a sigh of great relief, and they ran around the corner into the very busy street. Gary guided Lisa on to the stairs entrance of 'Debenhams' store, where it was quieter.

'Phew.' He flopped down on the concrete stairs and grinned up at Lisa. 'Don't look so worried – it's all right.'

'You were gone for ages. I thought . . . well, why were you so long? What did you say? Did you manage to sell the medal?'

'Hold on, hold on,' laughed Gary. 'I wasn't that long, not really. The old bloke was telling me about the medal, showing me some others. I told him it had belonged to my grandad, and he'd given it to me. I said I wanted to sell it to buy a present for my mum's birthday. Well, it's nearly true, isn't it?' he said defensively, catching Lisa's expression. 'I explained about my dad being dead and that, and all of a sudden he stopped

23

being suspicious and started telling me a lot of stuff about the war.'

'So what about the medal?'

Gary put his hand into his pocket and then moved to one side of the steps as a man and woman came down them. When they had gone, he drew out a ten pound note with a flourish.

'Ten pounds!' gasped Lisa.

Gary shrugged, trying to look casual, although he was clearly very excited. 'It's a . . . Naval General Service medal,' he said, screwing his face up in an effort to remember. 'And it's nearly a hundred and fifty years old!' He smiled. 'I think it's probably worth a lot more than that, but when he asked me how much I wanted, I just said my mum's present would be ten pounds. He gave me these as well, for myself.' In his other hand lay two shiny one pound coins.

'Oh, Gary!' said Lisa. Two or three pounds she could just about have coped with. But twelve pounds suddenly made it all seem really criminal, instead of a bit dishonest.

'So, time for a celebration, eh?' grinned Gary. 'We'll go and buy a feast to share with the Gang, and if Old Fogarty plays his cards right, I'll even invite him to join us, seeing as he's such a special friend of your family.'

Forgarty was often to be found at Lisa's house, complaining about the behaviour of various people or discussing his latest ideas for the neighbourhood; he was in charge of the Neighbourhood Watch scheme, and considered himself almost a part of the police force.

Lisa laughed and shoved Gary in the chest. 'Fool!' she said. But Gary winced with pain, and she stopped laughing. 'Are you all right? I didn't mean to hit you

24

that hard, Gary. I'm sorry.' Then her face darkened. 'I *didn't* hit you that hard. It's him again, isn't it?'

Gary didn't answer. 'Isn't it?' Lisa persisted.

Gary nodded.

'Let me see.'

Slowly, Gary started to unbutton his shirt. An elderly lady, making her way up the stairs, looked at him in disgust. 'Well really!' she said, but did not stop. Clearly she had decided Gary was a depraved young hooligan who might do anything if challenged. Normally this would have made them laugh, but this time they both just looked around to make sure she had gone, and there was no one else in sight. On Gary's chest, just over his lower ribs on the left, was a large blue bruise. The skin looked red and swollen round the edge of it.

Lisa swallowed. The savageness of hitting anyone, never mind a child, so hard was not easy for her to understand. 'What happened?' she whispered, as Gary pulled his shirt back over the injury.

'He'd been drinking,' he said bitterly.

'What, already? This morning, you mean?'

Gary nodded. 'It's getting worse,' he said. 'He never used to drink until after work.' Gary's uncle worked the afternoon shift at the dockyard. 'But lately he's taking to it in the mornings – and if he doesn't, he's so bad-tempered without it that it's almost as bad.'

'Did he just come up and hit you, without any reason?' asked Lisa, mystified.

'Oh he had a reason, all right,' said Gary. 'It was my turn to wash up after breakfast this morning, and I forgot. Well, actually, I didn't even forget. I was about to do it when Mum asked me to go to the shop, and by the time I got back he was up.'

'But didn't your mum do something?' asked Lisa,

trying to picture the scene. Her own mother would never allow anyone to hurt her like this, however much bigger and stronger they were.

'She tried to explain, but he wasn't in the mood to listen. Called me an idle bugger and thumped me. When I turned round to get away he said I was being cheeky and thumped me again.' Quickly he turned around and lifted his shirt. There was another bruise over his shoulder blade. Lisa touched it gently; it was not so dark and swollen as the other one, but it must have hurt.

'Gary, you've got to tell someone.'

'No.'

'Gary, listen to me. That bruise on your chest doesn't look right – what if you've broken a rib or something? You need to go to the doctor, and tell him the truth.'

'No.'

'Gary, please. Don't be stupid. If you tell someone, they'll have to do something.'

'Like what?' Gary's eyes creased scornfully at her silence. 'He says I deserve it. It's my word against his. My mum's just too scared and too worn down to know what's going on half the time. So what'll they do? Take me away? Put me in a children's home, p'raps? And then who'll look after my mum?'

Lisa looked down at the hard stone steps. She had no answer. Biting back the tears, she looked at Gary, small and crumpled on the edge of the stairs. Gently, she put her arms around him and hugged him. He patted her back, as though she was a little child. 'It'll be all right,' he soothed. 'Come on, Lisa. Don't go soft on me, eh? Write it all down in that diary of yours, yeah? And one day, if we have to, we'll get my mum out and then shop the old bully.'

26

Lisa pulled herself upright and sniffed. She nodded. Soon after Gary had confided in her, Lisa had come up with the idea of recording all the injuries Gary got from his uncle in her diary. Then, if ever he felt brave enough, or confident enough that his mother would not suffer, they could go to the police or whoever with a record of it all. At first, she had not told Gary, but then she had felt bad about it, as though she was keeping a secret file and spying on him. So she had told him that she was writing it all down – exactly what he told her, and a description of the marks. (The uncle never hit him anywhere it would show. It was a calculated sort of violence that made her shiver at the thought.) Once he knew the diary was well-hidden and wouldn't be found by her parents, Gary had just shrugged and said it was up to her. But he never volunteered any information about being ill-treated; it was always left to her to guess, and then persuade him to tell her. She never knew whether she guessed every time, or whether he was beaten more often than she knew. But it was better than standing by and doing nothing.

'Hey, Lisa? It's me that was thumped, and you that's doing the crying. Typical girl!'

She went to shove him again, but remembered in time and waved her hand in the air instead, looking haughty. 'You're not allowed to say that sort of thing nowadays, young man,' she joked. 'Equal whatsits – boys and girls are the same.'

'Could've fooled me,' said Gary, with a sly nudge.

They both laughed, feeling embarrassed and awkward. Then Gary straightened up and held out his hand, pulling Lisa to her feet. 'Let's go and choose the stuff,' he said.

The responsibility of the twelve pounds washed over

Lisa anew. Miserably, she followed Gary round the food hall. He bought Coca-Cola, crisps and some dark minty chocolates that he knew were her favourites. He also bought a cake in a box, and a big bargain pack of sweets. Lisa managed to stick a smile on her face whenever necessary, but she actually felt slightly sick. She couldn't wait to get home, right away from the whole thing.

As they got off the bus at Wood Lane, Lisa said, 'Look, Gary. I won't be able to come to the hut. Sorry – I've just remembered I promised Mum I'd clean my room out today. I'll have to do it, or she won't give me any pocket money.'

'Oh, come on. You can do your room tonight. It won't be so much fun without you,' said Gary.

Lisa flushed. 'Of course it will. And Mum made me promise to do it before dinner. Anyway, p'raps I can come out afterwards, if I get it done straight away. I'll see you later, OK?'

'OK,' said Gary reluctantly.

As Lisa walked away he called after her. 'Lisa?'

'Yes?' She turned around, and Gary thrust something into her hand, then ran off into the Tennesons' drive. He had given her the mint chocolates.

Lisa went straight upstairs and hid them in the bottom of her wardrobe, underneath the car racing set. She had never felt less hungry in her whole life.

Four

'What's the matter, Lisa?' said Mrs McBride at dinner-time. 'You haven't eaten a thing.' She laid a hand on Lisa's forehead. 'Do you feel ill?'

'No, Mum. I'm all right, honestly. I just don't feel hungry.'

'Lovers' tiff, I expect,' said Chris cheerfully. 'I'll have your pork chop, Sis.'

'Lovers' tiff?' echoed Mrs McBride. She caught the angry look Lisa directed at Chris over the table, and smiled. 'Oh, I see.'

'Did you have a good day, Mum? Was the flannel man there?' asked Lisa, to distract attention away from herself.

The story of the flannel man was an ever-continuing saga in the McBride house. Mum was a social worker, and one of her clients was an elderly man who never went anywhere without his little flannel blanket.

'Like a baby!' Lisa had exclaimed in disgust when she first saw him at Mum's office. But Mum had explained that he was quite ill, and his mind just didn't work in the same way as other people's.

'Mr Rodgers thinks the world will fall on top of him if he loses that blanket,' said Mum. 'Now just think. If *you* had charge of that blanket, and if you *knew*, for absolute certain, that the whole world would come to

29

an end if you lost it, what would you do? Would *you* let it out of your sight? It's a big responsibility.'

'But it's not true!' said Lisa, confused. 'It's just a silly old blanket.'

'Mr Rodgers doesn't see it that way. If you really want to understand, look at it from his point of view, as if it *were* true.'

When Lisa did try to imagine this, it was very scary. After that, Lisa thought about the old man all the time, even though she only saw him once more. She went with Dad to meet Mum from the office, and he was sitting in reception. His brown-rimmed glasses perched crookedly on a bony face, and his mac was crumpled. He rocked quietly to and fro, clutching the blanket to his chest. Lisa felt a bit scared of him, but she offered him one of her sweets, and smiled at him encouragingly as he took one. The flannel man smiled back. He had not stopped smiling all the time Lisa was there, just smiling and chewing.

'I won't be seeing Mr Rodgers, or the flannel man as you call him, until next week,' said Mum. 'He's doing well, though. He still asks about you. Every single time I see him, he says, "How's your little girl? The one who gave me the sweet," he says.' Mrs McBride sighed as she collected the empty plates. 'Poor man; I don't suppose many people would give him a sweet.'

'He sounds creepy,' said Chris. 'Daft as a brush.'

'Leave him alone!' shouted Lisa. 'He's got nobody. Nobody, only that old blanket. You've never seen him – you don't understand!'

Chris and Mum were looking at her in amazement.

'All right, love, calm down,' said Mum quietly. 'Ooh, by the way, we had a letter from Martin this morning.'

Martin was Lisa's eldest brother. He was at Exeter

30

University. Usually he came home for the holidays, and took a job at Debenhams in Plymouth, but this summer he was staying in Exeter. He had found a job there as a hospital porter, and would only be able to manage a few days at home. Lisa missed Martin more than she had ever thought it was possible to miss anybody. Not just because he could not take her out for the day or build her a go-kart, as he had done before. Martin would understand, about the flannel man, and Gary, and – oh, everything, if only he was here.

'Did he put a note in for me?' she asked eagerly.

Mum shook her head. 'No, not this time. He says he'll write again at the end of the week; this was just a short note to let us know he's going climbing for a couple of days, with a friend. He sends his love, though.'

'Oh,' said Lisa. She wished Martin had not stayed on in Exeter this summer. There was no one else she could share her troubles with. Feeling miserable, Lisa crept up to her bedroom and sat on the bed, hugging her old teddy. She imagined the Gang tucking in to their feast, without her. Sally-Anne would ask, 'Where's Lisa, then?' She would not believe Lisa was tidying her room.

Lisa did not understand why Sally-Anne hated her, but she knew it to be true. Dad had once said, when Lisa complained about her, 'Poor Sally-Anne. Always on the outside, looking in. No wonder her eyes are green.'

This made no sense at all to Lisa. For a start, Sally-Anne's eyes were blue. And she was not 'poor'. She was spiteful, and horrid.

There was a tap at the door, and Fliss poked her head in. 'Hello. Busy?'

'No. Come on in,' said Lisa, surprised.

She moved up on the bed and Lisa sprawled across it, flat on her back.

'I am so *full*, she groaned dramatically. 'Absolutely stuffed with food. That third piece of cake really was the end – and then my mum came up with the brilliant idea of spaghetti bolognese for dinner. Can you believe it?' She groaned again, rolling her eyes.

'Where are the others?' said Lisa. 'Still there?'

'No.' Fliss sat up and stretched. 'Gone home. Zeke's watching some old film. Otherwise he would have come, too. We want to tell you something.'

'Yes?' said Lisa.

Fliss looked embarrassed. 'Look, Lisa. Zeke and I feel bad about the whole thing. We should have stopped Gary from selling that stupid medal. You're right. It's not in the same league as scrumping apples off Old Fogarty, who doesn't want them in the first place. It's more than naughty kids. It's . . . it's. . . .'

'Criminal,' said Lisa carefully.

'Yes. I suppose it is,' agreed Fliss.

They sat in silence for a moment. Then Fliss pushed her hair out of her eyes and slammed her hands down on the bed.

'But,' she said, 'it is all over now. I mean, it's too late to do anything now. We'll know better next time. Let's forget the whole thing. OK?' She held out her palms.

'OK,' said Lisa, bringing her hands down on to Fliss's.

They chatted for a while, played a couple of games of 'snap', and then Fliss went home.

Lisa felt a lot better. At least Fliss and Zeke were on her side. Perhaps it was best just to forget the whole thing, like Fliss said. Gary was not a friend she wanted to risk losing. It was all over now, anyway.

But it was by no means over, not yet, as Lisa was soon to discover. When Dad came home that night, he settled in front of the television waiting for the news, as he always did after the day shift. Lisa sat on the floor, leaning against the itchy wool of his trousers and answering idle questions about her day here and there. As usual, she groaned when the news came on. It was so boring.

'Sssh,' said Dad. 'I'm working on this case.'

That sounded a bit more interesting. Lisa turned her attention to what the newscaster was saying:

'Police are still baffled about how the thieves managed to outsmart the elaborate security system at Thurlow Park, the home of wealthy Plymouth industrialist. . . .'

'That's right by us!' shouted Lisa. 'Just on the other side of the school field.'

'Be quiet!' hissed Dad impatiently.

'The haul in last night's robbery included several valuable paintings, one of them a portrait by Van Meer.'

A dull-looking picture of a man with lots of curls and a peculiar coat was flashed across the screen.

'The thieves appear to have simply walked in and out of the rooms quite freely, despite a burglar alarm system installed at a cost of over one hundred thousand pounds.'

'Wow,' said Lisa. 'Those paintings must have been worth a lot?' She looked enquiringly at her father.

Dad just nodded tersely at the screen. 'That's what they were really after,' he said grimly.

For a moment, Lisa thought she had yelped aloud when she looked back at the television. Medals – rows and rows of medals.

'. . . the largest collection of small military items in

Europe . . . some of them priceless . . . police are looking for any information . . . no idea who. . . .'

Lisa could not really follow the rest. Her head was swimming. She felt as if claws of ice had gripped at her heart.

'We're one step ahead of the press for a change,' Dad crowed to Mum. 'They obviously haven't heard, yet.'

'Heard what?' said Lisa.

Dad knocked his pipe on the ashtray and put some new tobacco into it. 'We had a lead this afternoon. One of the medals showed up.'

Lisa wished there was a volume control on heartbeats. Surely Mum and Dad could hear hers.

'Did it?' she asked, through dry lips.

'Yes. Young lad sold it to a shop in Plymouth. Bold as brass – just walked in and said it was his grandad's, apparently. The owner of the shop only put two and two together when he heard about the robbery.'

Lisa silently willed her father to go on speaking. She did not trust her voice to ask any more questions. If they saw how nervous she was, Mum and Dad would keep on until they knew the truth.

Dad puffed on his pipe for what seemed like ages, and then finally he said, 'Find the boy, find the gang.'

'How's that?' said Mum.

'We are working on the assumption that the lad was the lookout. He was given the medal – perhaps more than one – as a payment. It's not one of the really valuable ones, but it would fetch enough for a boy to be interested in. So we're putting our efforts into finding the boy. . . .'

'Lisa! Lisa, where are you going?' called Mum.

Lisa stopped at the door. 'I . . . forgot to tell Fliss something. I won't be a minute.'

As she opened the door, Dad called, 'be back before it gets too dark,' and then he must have raised his eyebrows at Mum the way he did when he wanted to know what was going on, because Lisa heard her mother say, 'she's been a bit odd all day. Chris reckons it's a boy, would you believe?'

Lisa slammed the door, and ran.

Five

It took a while to get the Gang together, and in the end they met without Sally-Anne. Her mother said it was too late for her to come out. Lisa was too worried even to enjoy the sight of Sally-Anne's furious face pressed up against the glass as the others hurried off to the hut together.

Daylight had already begun to fade as Zeke opened up the Headquarters. He switched on the lamp. It glowed orange in the gloom of the grey light filtering through the small window, and made everyone's faces look pale and peculiar.

Quickly, Lisa explained exactly what had happened. Fliss put her hands over her face, and Gary sank down onto the cushions. Zeke just stared at Lisa. 'Oh, no,' he said finally.

'Oh yes,' said Lisa. 'And we'd better work out what to do, fast. I have to be home before dark, or there'll be questions.'

They all looked at Gary, waiting for him to speak. He looked up at them, and fished in his pockets. 'I've got five pounds twenty left,' he said. 'What if I just sent it to your dad at the police station, with an anonymous note explaining exactly what happened?'

'Police have ways of tracing anonymous notes, if they really want to,' said Fliss. 'What about just owning up?'

'They might not believe me.'

'Lisa's dad would, surely,' said Fliss. 'Especially if Lisa told him about it, too.'

All eyes turned towards Lisa. 'I don't know,' she said, confused. 'I mean, yes, I'm sure Dad would believe Gary. But I don't know if that's enough. They'll have lots of people working on it, not just Dad. You might have to convince the others as well. I just don't know what would happen.'

'Anyway,' said Zeke slowly. 'Gary did sell the medal, didn't he, even though he knew it wasn't his? That must be what they call handling stolen property. It's a crime, isn't it? From the police point of view, I mean,' he finished, catching sight of Gary's expression.

Gary's face looked ghastly in the grey-orange light. 'But I didn't know it was stolen,' he said. 'Some people say it's "Finders, Keepers".'

'The police don't,' said Lisa miserably. 'Not when it's something valuable, anyway.'

'Lisa, if Gary didn't know, does that make a difference? To the police, I mean?'

'How should I know?' snapped Lisa. 'My dad's the policeman, not me. You expect me to know everything!'

She felt tears pricking at the back of her eyelids, waiting for a chance to fall. She wanted to say, 'I told Gary not to do it. I knew there'd be trouble,' but there was no point and anyway, she had not tried very hard to stop him, had she? She'd even helped him, in a way. So she just said, 'Do you know all about writing television plays, just because your dad is a writer?'

Zeke was rubbing his thumb thoughtfully. 'No, of course not. I'm sorry. But the trouble is, if we don't know how serious it is, what Gary has done, we can't really decide what to do. You see?'

'I feel sick,' moaned Gary. He put his head down

onto his knees, and Lisa saw him wince. His chest was still hurting.

'I know,' said Zeke. 'Why don't you get your dad talking about the *idea* of finding something and selling it. Ask what would happen *if* a child did what Gary did. . . .'

'But don't mention my name,' put in Gary quickly.

'Yes, that's a good idea,' said Fliss, suddenly enthusiastic. 'We'll meet tomorrow morning and work out what to do when we have all the information.'

'He'll suspect something,' said Lisa. 'You don't get to be a detective inspector by being stupid, you know. He's got a nose for trouble,' she said, remembering a remark the sergeant at the desk had once made. 'And I can't lie to him – he always knows,' she finished, wanting nothing more to do with it.

'If he looks at all suspicious you'll have to stop, of course,' said Zeke. 'But we really do need to know, don't we? And you're the only one who can find out.'

'Please, Lisa,' said Gary. 'Find out if there's a way out of this without my mum getting to know.' There was a slight quaver in his voice which tore at her. She knew that it was not his mother he was worried about. What would his uncle do to him, if Gary owned up? She remembered the bruises from 'forgetting' to do the washing up.

'All right.' She turned away quickly, not looking at him. 'I've got to go now – it's dark already. 'Bye.' Lisa pushed open the door and picked her way through the darkness. It was not fair of them to make her do this, she thought. Tomorrow she would tell them so – and she would find better things to do with her time than go around with a stupid Gang, too. Meanwhile, Lisa wondered how on earth she was going to strike up a casual conversation which would bring Dad round to what she wanted him to talk about. It was not going to be easy.

Lisa's step slowed as she reached the end of the Tennesons' front drive. Fogarty was there, waiting for her. He waved a gnarled finger.

'I know what you've been up to, don't think I don't. Disgraceful. Disgraceful, the way children are allowed to behave nowadays.'

'Hello, Mr Fogarty. What on earth do you mean?' asked Lisa politely, her heart thumping.

'No? No. Little Miss Innocence? Then why is your face red as a strawberry? Eh? Tell me that. Eh?' Old Fogarty was almost dancing in triumph.

How could he know? Frantically, Lisa went over the day's events in her mind, trying to spot a clue Fogarty could have picked up. She did not see how he could have found out anything at all, unless. . . .

'You've been listening at the door!' she shouted astonished. 'Creeping into the garden – the Tennesons' garden – and listening in!'

'What? What d'you say? Don't be daft, girl.' The beady green eyes shone in the withered face. He looked just like a hawk watching its prey. 'Listen at the door? That's your guilty conscience speaking, my girl. I don't need to be listening at doors. I saw the evidence with my own eyes!'

'What evidence?' For one wild moment, Lisa thought the old man must have followed them into Plymouth, and watched Gary sell the medal.

'Footprints!' crowed Fogarty. 'Footprints all over my fresh potting compost – and you've ruined my sweetpeas. You ought to be ashamed.'

The apples. He was only talking about the apples.

Lisa's stomach returned to normal, and she almost giggled.

'I don't expect any better from the children of arty types like her,' Old Fogarty sniffed and jerked his head towards the Tennesons' house. 'But you! A policeman's daughter should know better.'

Lisa was so relieved that he had not discovered the real crime, she let this pass. Old Fogarty waved his finger at her again.

'You tell your little friends that if I find any sound or sign of you in my garden again, there'll be trouble.'

He leaned forward. Lisa could smell onions on his breath. 'Especially for you, I should think, your dad being what he is.'

Lisa looked him straight in the eye. 'I'm afraid I don't know what you're talking about, Mr Fogarty, but I will pass on the message,' she said coolly. Then she walked away. Lisa could feel the beady eyes boring into her back.

'What happened to you?' Mr McBride was waiting at the door. 'You should have been back long ago.'

'Sorry, Dad. I was only talking with Fliss.'

'Hmm,' said her dad. 'That's not the point. You know I don't like you outside after dark. I've seen too much of what can happen to a young girl.'

'Dad! I was only four doors away — not even out of sight of the house.' Lisa felt a sulky expression begin to settle on her face, and could not stop it.

'Don't take that tone with me,' said Dad. 'Now go and get ready for bed. And next time I say before dark, just you make sure it is before dark, young lady.'

'Honestly!' muttered Lisa under her breath. She tossed her head and flounced up the stairs. There would be no cosy chat tonight.

It was a long time before Lisa could get to sleep, and then her dreams were unpleasant. The flannel man was in the medal shop, and he had swopped his blanket for the medal. Now he was hunting for it, to get it back again. He didn't trust Gary to look after it properly. Lisa could see his beady eyes clearly, behind the crooked glasses. He pushed his face close to hers, staring; staring and chewing. 'Where is he? Where is my blanket?' the flannel man kept asking. 'It's the end, you know. It's the end.'

Lisa woke with a start. For a moment she was convinced the flannel man was really there, standing over her bed. But it was only the shadow cast by the moonlight pouring through the window. Still shaking, Lisa jumped out of bed and drew her curtains across. The room was totally dark now. Usually, Lisa liked to watch the moon and stars through her window, and she liked the early morning sun waking her in the morning. But tonight she wanted to hide away from everyone, even the light.

Breakfast the next morning gave Lisa her chance. It was a very relaxed meal for once. Mum had a case conference in the civic centre at ten o'clock, and did not have to go into the office. Chris, who had been out late the night before, would probably not emerge until midday.

'Right, Lisa,' said Dad. 'I've got until lunchtime to mess about doing nothing, after I've washed up from breakfast. How about a walk on the beach – see how many crabs we can catch?'

Lisa loved walking on the beach, especially with Dad all to herself. The rock pools at Wembury, just a short drive away, stretched for miles when the tide was out, and Dad seemed to know the names of everything in them.

For a moment, she was tempted. Why not? she thought. Gary had been stupid – let him sort it out himself. She didn't see why she should stick her neck out. All the same . . . she remembered Gary's face on Debenhams' staircase, and the box of chocolates. 'It won't be the same without you. . . .' The truth was, if it had been anyone else she would probably have gone to Wembury. But Gary needed her, and she was the only one who really understood what life was like for him. She couldn't let him down.

'Dad, I can't. I promised the others I'd see them this morning. We're playing this game, and they need me.'

Dad looked quite surprised, but he said nothing, just picked up his pipe from the table and knocked the old tobacco out.

Mr McBride disciplined himself not to smoke during the day, but he always had the pipe with him. It was a great joke with Chris and Lisa. Today, though, she didn't tease him as he put the empty pipe in his mouth and picked up the newspaper.

'Dad?' Lisa's heart was thumping again.

'Mmmm?'

'That boy who sold the medal. Is he a criminal? I mean, what if he didn't get it from the robbery. What if he just found it?'

Dad snorted behind his newspaper. ' "I found it on the floor, Sir",' he mimicked. ' "Honest, Sir!" I wish I had a pound for every time I've heard that one.'

Lisa hung her head. 'But if a child *were* to find something, and keep it – or sell it. Would that be a crime? Would they go to prison?' Lisa held her breath. Her cheeks were flaming, but Dad was still behind the news-paper.

'Certainly,' he said promptly. 'Thirty years at least. They'd probably throw away the key.'

'George, she's being serious,' said Mum. 'Just look at her.'

Mr McBride lowered his paper and they both stared at Lisa. Dad leaned over the table towards her. 'What's the matter, baby?'

'Nothing,' said Lisa. 'And I'm not a baby. I wish you'd stop calling me that.' She wanted to cry again.

'Lisa, are you in trouble? Are you worried about something?' Dad was watching her very closely. He took her hand, but Lisa shook it away.

'No, I haven't done anything. Is this the way you interrogate your suspects at work?' she asked coldly. 'I just think it's a bit daft to go hunting a little boy who's probably done nothing wrong. You'd think the police would be able to catch a few robbers without hounding innocent children.'

'It's a pity you're not in charge of the investigation then, isn't it?' said Dad, tight-lipped.

This was Lisa's cue to say sorry. Dad was only trying to help her, she could see that. But if she opened her mouth again she was going to burst into tears. So she just pushed back her chair and went to the door.

'Lisa, come here.'

'Leave her, George.' She heard Mum's quiet voice. 'Life's all a bit much for her just now.'

Slowly, Lisa climbed the stairs. She could hear the murmur of voices in the kitchen. No doubt Mum was telling Dad all about the difficulties of being a girl growing into womanhood. It was one of her favourite topics, and she did a lot of work with teenage girls. She

43

would also tell him about the boy that Chris believed was at the root of it, though neither of them realized he was talking about Gary. Normally, Lisa would have had a good giggle with Fliss about that. But it did not seem at all funny now. It just made it more difficult to tell the truth. Lisa had not found out anything. The Gang were right back to square one.

Six

Later that morning, a gloomy silence settled inside the hut. Everyone was there except Gary; they just waited, saying nothing. Even Sally-Anne was too dispirited to insult Lisa as usual. No one knew what to say.

'It's school next week,' said Fliss at last.

'So?' Zeke looked puzzled.

'Well, they only have to take this old man to the schools, don't they? So he can pick out the boy who sold him the medal – Gary.' Fliss started chewing her thumb nail.

'There are loads of schools, though. The police won't know whereabouts Gary comes from. Besides,' Lisa tried to sound cheerful, 'he's very small for his age. They'll probably start with the junior schools – and we'll be at Lee Moor High.'

Lisa had looked forward to the first day of school, no longer a brand-new pupil. Her uniform hung ready, cleaned and pressed, in the wardrobe. Several times, Lisa had got it out and held it against herself, imagining what it would be like to be an old hand, showing the nervous newcomers around the school. All the pleasure had now been overshadowed by worries about what would happen when the truth came out, as it must in the end.

It would not be a good start with the teachers, some of whom were new. They would not trust Lisa and

Gary, when they heard what they had done. Probably no one would trust them. It would be no good Lisa saying she had not wanted to go with Gary, either. She had gone, and still had the mint chocolates. Dad would call it being an accomplice.

'Zeke, what do you think we should do?' asked Fliss.

Zeke, being the oldest and the leader, felt he should come up with something, but clearly didn't know what. 'We should . . . we have to . . . what we really need is someone to talk to. A grown-up who knows the law, but can be trusted to keep a secret.'

'Huh!' said Sally-Anne. 'That rules out all the grown-ups I know.'

'Martin!' shouted Lisa suddenly.

They all looked at her.

'Martin can be trusted,' she grinned.

'Martin's in Exeter,' said Sally-Anne.

Zeke's face brightened. 'That's it! Lisa and Gary can go to Exeter, find Martin, and tell him all about it. If they go early, they can be back by teatime, and no one need know.'

'Yes,' said Fliss. 'We can say we're all going on a picnic or something – except that Lisa and Gary will have their picnic on the train!'

'Martin will know what to do,' said Zeke, and Lisa smiled at him. She felt proud.

'We can't go today, though. Or tomorrow – at least I don't think so,' she said, suddenly remembering the letter he had written. 'He's gone climbing for a couple of days. And anyway, he might be at work when we get there. There's no phone, so we can't even let him know we're coming.' Lisa's face fell. It had all seemed so hopeful when she first thought of it.

'We'll just have to make it . . . Friday, then,' Zeke

46

calculated. 'If Martin's not in, you'll just have to wait. And hope he's not on a day shift. You'll just have to risk it.'

Lisa nodded.

Fliss looked a bit more hopeful. 'At least we've got the train fare,' she said. 'The leftover money should cover it.'

Suddenly, Zeke jumped to his feet. 'There's someone outside,' he whispered. They all froze. Footsteps approached the door and then stopped. Slowly the door opened. It was Gary.

'You forgot the password,' said Sally-Anne. 'You scared us half to death. We thought it was the – what's the matter?'

Gary looked ill. His skin was grey and his eyes were huge. A grimy trail led from his red-rimmed eyes down the thin cheeks. There was a red mark just below one eye, beginning to swell up.

'Gary, are you all right?' asked Fliss. 'What happened? Here, come and sit down.' She led Gary to the bathroom stool.

'He found it,' said Gary. 'The old pig found my money.'

'Who? What?' asked Zeke.

'Uncle Jack. He barged into my room to tell me off about something or other, and saw it lying on the dresser.'

'Oh, no! What did you say?' Fliss was wide-eyed.

'I said it was club funds, but he didn't believe me. He said I must have pinched it, and he kept asking me who I'd stolen it from.' Gary fingered the bruise that was beginning to appear on his cheek.

'He didn't . . . he didn't *hit* you!' said Fliss, white-faced. Lisa looked around at the faces of her friends.

They were completely shocked. She had often wondered if they, like her, had suspected that Gary was beaten by his uncle, but she could see now that they had had no idea. Zeke stood absolutely rigid, his fists clenched by his sides. Sally-Anne, whose parents were considered the strictest, was about to cry; even her parents would never hit her in the face. Fliss and Zeke, who were rarely even told off seriously, were outraged.

Lisa knelt beside Gary, and asked him, 'Is that all there is, Gary? Did he hit you anywhere else?'

'For heaven's sake, Lisa – isn't this enough?' shouted Fliss, astonished at her friend's calmness.

Gary shook his head. 'No – I ran off before he could get me again. What am I going to do? What he's done so far is nothing to what'll happen if the police come round.'

'Wait a minute,' said Zeke. 'You mean, your uncle's done this sort of thing before?'

Gary looked at Lisa, and she took his hand, just briefly, because she was embarrassed at showing her feelings for him in front of the others. Gary's head was bowed, and she knew he felt humiliated. None of it was his fault, and yet he felt ashamed. Lisa had never experienced real hate before, but she hated Gary's uncle for doing that to him. She waited for Gary to speak, and when he didn't, she said simply, 'This isn't the first time. Let's leave it at that.'

'You knew then?' Zeke's eyes as he looked at Lisa were wide.

She nodded, and watched Zeke struggle not to ask more.

Sally-Anne opened her mouth to speak, but Zeke, anticipating her, kicked her foot and she was silent. No one knew what to say, or do. The sight of Gary looking

48

so defeated and forlorn, and the thought that he had been suffering abuse from his uncle all this time without anyone knowing, except Lisa, silenced them all for a while.

'Listen, Gary,' said Zeke at last. 'Lisa had an idea.' He explained the plan to find Martin, and Gary looked gratefully at Lisa.

'I don't have any money now, though,' he said. 'Well, only fifty pence that was in my trousers pocket.'

'We'll get the money somehow,' said Zeke. 'We have until Friday.'

'If the police don't find him first,' said Sally-Anne.

They hadn't thought of this.

'Look,' said Gary, 'all they can possibly do is bring the old bloke down to the area of the robbery and see if he recognizes someone. If I stay off the streets, I can't get caught. So I'll just hide here until Friday. Then Uncle Jack can't get me, either.'

'What? Don't be daft – that's two days and two nights away. You can't just disappear!' said Lisa incredulously.

'Don't see why not,' said Gary. 'I'll leave a note for my mum, tell her not to worry. She won't call the police. She's too scared to leave the house these days. She's got agoraphobia. *He* won't bother coming to look for me. He'll be too worried I've told someone about him belting me.'

'What's agoraphobia?' said Sally-Anne.

'Fear of going outside,' said Gary.

'That makes it even worse if you go missing, can't you see?' Lisa felt as though she was dealing with a small, silly child, not someone her own age. 'She'll be worried, and not be able to look for you. That's cruel, Gary.'

'Not half as cruel as if the police find me before we have a chance to sort it all out,' said Gary defiantly. 'No, I'm going to lie low, just until Friday. We'll do whatever Martin says.'

'You're talking as though Martin knows everything about everything,' argued Lisa. 'What if he doesn't know what to do, either? He might just tell you to own up. He might not be able to come up with a single thing we haven't thought of already.'

'He has to,' said Gary simply.

They talked for a long time, going round and round in circles. Fliss and Lisa thought Gary should go home and face up to his uncle. It was very unlikely that Gary would be connected with the robbery by his Uncle Jack. Privately, Lisa thought he should just own up and put a stop to the whole silly mess. There was no point in saying this aloud. Gary was determined not to go home, and Zeke and Sally-Anne supported him.

'He might get beaten again,' said Zeke indignantly.

Lisa could see that he, of all of them, was the most affected by this. Zeke, for all his strength as leader of the Gang, was a very kind and gentle boy at heart. His parents had probably never had much reason to be cross with him. On the rare occasions when they were, their tactics tended to be withdrawing pocket money or treats. Some parents shouted, some smacked. Gary's uncle had gone too far, but it wasn't as bad for Gary as it would be for Zeke. She attempted to explain this to him. 'Look, it's not really as bad as. . . .'

Gary turned to look at her. His eye was beginning to close. It made Lisa wince just to look at it. She had to admit there was a big difference between a clip round the ear and this sort of injury, or the one to his chest. 'All right, all right, I agree,' she said. 'We have to hide him.' She and Fliss were going to be outvoted anyway. It was better for them all to work together than to quarrel. Gary needed help.

There was another discussion about the best place for Gary to hide. The hut was their first idea. It was ideal, apart from the fact that it was close to home. They thought about a few other places, but always came back to the hut. It was private. It was dry. The Gang would be able to get food and drink to him, and there was a bed. There was nowhere better.

What about washing – and going to the loo?' asked Sally-Anne.

She may be the youngest, but Lisa had to admit that when it came to it, it was always Sally-Anne who could be relied on to see the problems.

'When the coast is clear in our house he can come in,' said Fliss. 'Otherwise, he'll have to use the garden. We'll have to keep an eye on Dad. He prowls about a bit when he's working. But when he goes to the gallery to pick Mum up, Gary can come in then.'

'I'll have a look for the clothes I grew out of last year,' said Zeke. 'I expect they'll fit. So there's no problem there.'

Lisa and Fliss exchanged tired glances. It was becoming almost an adventure. They seemed to be the only ones who didn't find it exciting.

Gary wrote a note to his mum, saying he was staying with a friend for a couple of days, 'until Uncle Jack cools down,' he wrote. He added, 'In Ivybridge. Don't worry. Back Saturday.'

'You don't know anyone in Ivybridge, do you?' asked Lisa.

'No. But Mum doesn't know that. And Ivybridge is

51

quite a long way away. It will stop her coming to your house, or Zeke's.'

Zeke offered to drop the letter through Gary's door later that day.

'Now all that's settled,' said Fliss, 'we must find something to do that will keep us out of everyone's way for as long as possible. I'll get the Monopoly set.' She set off for the house.

'Monopoly?' said Zeke. He shook his head. 'We're hiding a criminal on the run, and all she can think of to do is play Monopoly?'

They all laughed. No one thought it was funny, but it was a relief to have something to laugh at.

'Please hurry, Friday,' whispered Lisa as she cupped the dice ready to throw her turn. 'And don't let Gary get caught before we find Martin.'

Seven

The Gang stayed in the hut all day, going home only for lunch. Everyone managed to bring something for Gary, and he ate sandwiches, jam tart and an apple. There was an air of excitement and nervousness. No one wanted to leave, knowing that Gary would be on his own long enough, once the night came. They played Monopoly and cards, and then Monopoly again. A rap on the door gave them a scare – it was Mrs Tenneson, but she did not come in.

Zeke stood in the doorway, blocking her view of Gary crouching in the corner. 'Hello, Mum. What do you want?'

The others heard her laugh. 'Don't worry,' she said. 'I haven't come to pry into your secrets.'

Lisa could imagine the brown eyes sparkling as she looked at Zeke. Mrs Tenneson seemed to find everything amusing, especially her children. Even her hair was crinkled as if it was doubled up over a good joke. The Gang all loved her. They often forgot she was old, and the mother of Fliss and Zeke.

'What on earth you can be finding to do in there that's better than being outside on a day like this, I cannot imagine. But since you *are* here – can I speak to Gary, please?'

Everybody held their breath.

'Gary?' said Zeke. 'Er . . . Gary's not here. Matter of

fact, we haven't seen him all day. What do you want him for?'

'I don't want him particularly. I just need a child, and he's about the right size. Ah well – you'll have to do, Zeke. Will you come in for half an hour or so?'

'Oh Mum, not now!'

Mrs Tenneson often asked one of the children to model for her. She did quite a lot of work for a big chocolate manufacturer, designing calendars and chocolate box lids. Lisa had been very excited, the first time she had been asked to 'sit', and could not understand why Fliss and Zeke were not keen. She had been very quiet and still, and watched Mrs Tenneson working away with mounting excitement. Then, when Lisa had finally given up hope of ever being able to move again, Mrs Tenneson had said, 'Finished!' and swung round the easel so that Lisa could have a look.

It had not looked any different from the peculiar pictures the gallery sold; it did not even look like a girl, let alone Lisa. Nor could she see the flowers Mrs Tenneson had placed in her arms, or the hard peacock chair she had sat on all this time.

'Oh, it's lovely,' she had said, feeling cheated and cross.

Mrs Tenneson, not fooled, had laughed. 'Children are such Philistines – you'll be proud of it when you're older, you know.'

Lisa had smiled politely, taken the box of chocolates Mrs Tenneson had offered her, and escaped as soon as possible.

No one in the Gang was particularly keen to model for Mrs Tenneson at the best of times, and especially not today. Zeke was mumbling an excuse when they heard his mother say, 'Tell you what – I'll give you two pounds, if you sit for an hour.'

'All right,' said Zeke at once. 'I'll be there in a minute.'

He shut the door and tied up the shoes he had kicked off. 'That's a stroke of luck,' he said. 'Two children's returns to Exeter comes to . . . five pounds eighty,' he calculated. 'I went with Dad last week. So that'll be only three pounds eighty to find. See you later – keep the door locked, just in case.'

Zeke tossed the key to Fliss, and she locked the door from the inside when he had gone. Lisa began to feel like a trapped animal.

'This is daft,' she said. 'If anyone does come looking for Gary, they're bound to be suspicious. Here we are, all Gary's friends, locked in the hut together. We should all be out there somewhere, separated, so no one is surprised to find out we don't know where Gary is.'

It would have been lovely on the beach. Lisa wondered if Dad had gone alone, and whether he'd find any crabs. She pictured the cool sea, sparkling in the sun as the white-tipped waves danced onto the beach. The hut was so hot and stuffy, and her head hurt. 'This is daft,' she said again, more to herself than anyone else.

'I think you've got a point,' said Sally-Anne, much to Lisa's surprise. 'But we can't leave Gary alone, not at a time like this.'

'I don't mind,' said Gary. But they all knew he did. There was an embarrassed silence.

'There's eighty-two pence in the subs,' said Lisa, indicating the jar where they saved odd pennies for grand feasting celebrations. 'Call it eighty pence – where are we going to get the other three pounds?'

'I've got fifty pence with me,' said Gary, holding up

the coin. 'But we should maybe keep that for emergencies – phone calls, things like that.'

'That's right,' agreed Fliss. 'Zeke has done his bit, sitting for Mum, and Gary can't get any more. So that leaves Lisa, Sally-Anne and me. We have to raise one pound each. All right?'

The girls nodded. Lisa thought it shouldn't be too difficult to get that much out of her mum. Her parents often gave her extra pocket money in the school holidays, anyway. Mum just handed it over, but Dad always asked what it was for. Lisa hated the thought of lying to either of them, so she decided to ask Mum the next time they were alone.

'Can I have a pound?' she asked as her mother was clearing dinner that night. Dad was still at work, and Chris was tuning in to his stereo, having wasted precious time eating.

'Ask your dad when he comes in, will you? I've only got a ten pound note. I've got to go now. I'll be late. 'Bye, love.'

Mrs McBride aimed a kiss at Lisa's cheek, landed it just short of her ear, and took her jacket off the hook on the door.

'Where are you going?' asked Lisa.

'Training session for new voluntary workers,' said Mum. 'We're having an information film and a discussion about the new good neighbour service we're trying to set up.'

Lisa watched her mother check her handbag: purse, keys, diary. Zeke had planned to drop the letter through Gary's door about now. His mother and uncle would be in the back room, watching the early news on the television, as always. Gary often missed dinner, and they would not have begun to wonder about him yet.

Lisa tried to imagine what they would do. Perhaps the uncle would come looking for Gary. He would try all his friends, perhaps, starting with the closest. She pictured Gary's bruised face, and touched her own cheek.

'Mum, do you have to go?' she called suddenly.

Mrs McBride stopped in her tracks at the front door and came back. 'I'm afraid so,' she said. 'I'm in charge of the programme, you see? But Chris is here, and Dad won't be too late. I haven't much on tomorrow – we'll do something special then, if you like. Night night, darling.'

With another kiss, this one landing firmly on Lisa's nose, Mrs McBride was gone.

Lisa knew she should really go back to the hut. There was another couple of hours before dark, and they should stick together. But she could not bear the thought of that stuffy, closed-up hut which had been so cosy. She was scared, too, of what the uncle would do if he found Gary there.

When the doorbell rang, a few minutes later, Lisa stiffened. She crept towards the back door. If it was the police, or Gary's Uncle Jack, she would slip out. Lisa waited, her hand poised over the door handle. Chris did not come down the stairs. The doorbell rang again.

'Blast!' said Lisa under her breath. Chris must have his headphones on. Better not answer it, perhaps? They might think there was no one at home.

The doorbell rang a third time, loud and persistent. Someone knew the house was not empty.

Feeling quite sick and a bit giddy, Lisa went into the hallway. She could see a blurred figure through the frosted glass of the front door. It was too small to be a policeman, or Gary's uncle. Lisa opened the door.

Gary's mother stood on the step. One hand gripped the frame. Her eyes were wide and frightened, and she breathed very slowly and carefully, as though the simple business of taking one breath after another was difficult for her.

'Mrs Harvey,' said Lisa. 'What did you want? Um — I mean, do you want to come in?'

She opened the door a little wider, reluctantly beckoning the woman inside. Mrs Harvey shook her head. She seemed to be stuck to the spot. 'I'm looking . . . looking for Gary,' she said. 'Is he here?'

'No,' said Lisa. 'Sorry.'

Mrs Harvey looked as though she had been told Gary was lost at sea and never coming back. She flattened herself against the wall and closed her eyes for a moment. 'Do you know . . . where he is?'

'No,' said Lisa. 'I've no idea. Try the park. . .' she began, but the mention of the park made Mrs Harvey worse; she actually began to shake. Lisa could have kicked herself. Gary had said she was dead scared of being out in the open.

'Or Sally-Anne's house,' she added quickly, and began to shut the door.

'Lisa, what's going on?' said Chris behind her.

'Nothing,' said Lisa, praying her face would not start to burn. It did — she must be scarlet.

Chris put his hand on the door and pulled it open. Mrs Harvey was still standing there, flat against the wall, with her eyes firmly closed.

Chris looked at Mrs Harvey and then at Lisa. Lisa shook her head.

'I don't know what's the matter,' she whispered. 'She's looking for Gary. She's got agger . . . agrobe . . . something.'

'Agoraphobia?' asked Chris, and Lisa nodded.

'Mrs Harvey?' Chris went out to Gary's mum and put his hand on her arm. 'Mrs Harvey, I'll come back with you. It's all right. Just breathe slowly. Don't be afraid. I'll come with you, all right?'

Lisa had never seen Chris so gentle before. It made her want to cry. She seemed to cry a lot, just lately.

'Come on,' said Chris. They moved off down the path together. 'Send Dad down to Gary's house,' Chris called over his shoulder, 'if I'm not back when he gets home.'

Lisa nodded. She went back inside and sat on the seat by the dining room window, watching Chris and Mrs Harvey make their way slowly across the road and down Elderberry Walk. The Harveys lived right down at the other end. Poor Mrs Harvey must have been terrified.

Even when they were out of sight, Lisa kept watching. Finally, Dad's car drew up and she rushed out to meet him, explaining that he was needed at the Harveys' house. Then she washed up the dinner things, wiped the table, even cleaned the cooker. Still Chris and Dad were not back. Lisa made a pot of tea.

It was dark now. Lisa switched on the television. A row of smiling faces mocked her from the screen — it was some sort of show, and brightly-clothed dancers smiled and smiled as they whirled around.

Lisa heard the front door close, and she rushed into the hall.

'Is she all right?' she asked eagerly.

Chris looked at her very strangely and then went upstairs. The stereo started up, not quite as loud as usual.

Lisa's heart sank when she caught her father's eye.

59

He was not so much looking at her as searching her. For one awful moment, she thought he might be reading her mind.

'Come in here,' he said.

Lisa followed him into the living room and sat down, picking up a comic from the coffee table to hide her face in. Mr McBride turned the television off and took the comic away.

'Lisa, did you know Gary had gone missing?'

'Missing?' Lisa could feel him watching her, very closely. She did not look up.

'Have you seen Gary today?'

Lisa shook her head. 'He didn't come to the hut,' she said.

'Well, he's gone. Apparently there was some trouble with the uncle – but I suppose you wouldn't know anything about that, either?'

Lisa met his eyes for a moment and then looked away.

'Mrs Harvey's worried sick,' Dad went on. 'Gary's left some sort of crazy note and run away. She thinks something terrible will happen to him. Where is he, Lisa?'

'How should I know?' said Lisa. 'He's hardly likely to tell me, is he? Not the copper's kid,' she added bitterly. 'That's what they call me, you know.'

'Lisa!' She could see this remark had scored home. It was at least a way of distracting him from asking further questions, and Lisa carried on.

'You treat everybody as though they were a suspect,' she said. 'That's why no one really trusts me, not even the Gang, not really. We're friends all right – good friends, most of the time. But if they're up to something risky, they're not likely to tell me anything. It's far simpler to leave the copper's kid out altogether.'

There was in fact only a grain of truth in this; it was very rare that Lisa was left out because of the risk of her father finding out things the Gang would rather keep secret. Now Lisa realized how hurt and angry she was that it had ever happened at all.

Mr McBride sighed. 'Look, Lisa, just tell me: do you know where Gary is? A simple yes or no. If you tell me you don't know, I'll believe you. I know you don't tell lies.'

'You're behaving just like a policeman!' shouted Lisa. '*No one* likes policemen, and no one trusts policemen's children. Don't you understand that? Leave me alone. I haven't *done* anything!'

'You haven't answered my question, either,' said Mr McBride doggedly. 'Do you know where Gary is, or not?'

'No! No! Now just leave me alone!' Lisa ran out of the room and stormed up the stairs into her bedroom. She undressed and pulled on her pyjamas, clambered into bed and buried herself under the quilt. She half-expected Dad to follow her, but he didn't. Lisa heard him going into the kitchen, heard the pipes rumble as he filled the kettle. The tea Lisa had made for him would be cold by now.

Chris went downstairs. Lisa could hear the murmur of their voices below her. She lay awake in the darkness, wondering what had happened in Gary's house. Chris and Dad were surely talking about that. Still no one came up to see her.

Lisa rolled over and tried to sleep, but it was no use. Every time she closed her eyes, she saw a terrified Mrs Harvey, white-faced and shaking; saw her as clearly as if she were in the room. Or she saw the flannel man, rocking to and fro with his blanket, frightened of the world he believed was soon to end.

'It's all your stupid fault, Gary Harvey,' she muttered, pounding the mattress. 'It's all your own stupid fault.' She sobbed as quietly as she could into her pillow. If only she'd told Dad about it all, right at the beginning, before Gary even sold the medal.

'He wasn't here,' a voice reminded her. 'Nor was Mum. They're never here when you really need them, never.' Although this was quite untrue, it made Lisa feel even more sorry for herself, and started up new tears.

The front door slammed. Mum was home. Lisa stopped crying and rearranged her bedclothes. She practised taking slow, regular breaths and put her face in the crook of her arm, just as she did when she was asleep.

Sure enough, Mum opened the door and came in. Lisa couldn't see her, but she could smell the mixture of fresh night air and perfume, right by the bed.

'Lisa, are you awake?'

Lisa lay quite still, breathing hard.

'I think you are,' said Mum.

Still Lisa did not move.

'Lisa, Gary's mother has called the police. It will be an official investigation. You think about that. Think what that poor woman must be going through. Then think about telling Daddy and me what this is all about, eh? Eh, Lisa?'

Lisa felt her mother's hand stroking her head. 'Night night, darling,' she said, and went out.

More tears started to trickle in an itchy stream down the inside of Lisa's elbow. One by one, the sounds of the day petered out. The vibration from Chris's record player stopped, then the television downstairs. The kettle was put on for the last time, chairs scraped across the floor. Doors were closed, plugs pulled out. Mum and Dad came upstairs together. Taps ran in the bathroom, the loo flushed. Then the bedroom door closed and there was silence.

Lisa had closed the curtains, and the room was pitch dark. She held her eyes tightly closed and could see nothing. Nothing, except Mrs Harvey's terrified face, which seemed to float above her. The flannel man came back, whenever Lisa dozed off.

'Where is he? Where is he? He's got it, hasn't he? It's the end, the end.' The big eyes behind the broken glasses stared at her, unblinking, never blinking once.

'Shut up. Go away,' thought Lisa. 'It's nothing to do with you.'

'Where is he? Where *is* he?'

'He hasn't *got* your blanket!' Lisa was speaking aloud now. 'Go away. It's only the medal he's lost, not the blanket. . . .'

Then she dozed, and dreamed Gary was going into the shop all over again. But this time he was selling the blanket.

'No!' she shouted, and was instantly awake. Someone must have heard her. But the night was still and silent. The darkness sat all around her, watching, somehow accusing. You lied, Lisa, it seemed to say. Poor Mrs Harvey. Poor, terrified woman. And you lied.

It was almost light before Lisa slept again, and then Dad's alarm woke her after only an hour. The night was finally over. The day brought its own problems. What was she going to tell Mum and Dad?

Eight

Lisa had hoped to get out of the house before anyone else was up, and talk to Fliss and Zeke. When she came down the stairs, however, her parents were waiting, sitting at the dining-room table with the door wide open. They both saw her as she reached the foot of the stairs. Lisa felt her face stiffening like a plaster cast. She knew she looked sulky, and it was bound to irritate Dad. She just couldn't help it.

'Lisa, lovey, this is serious,' he said as Lisa sat down and poured cornflakes into her bowl. 'Mrs Harvey has reported Gary missing. She asked me to phone the station while I was there. If you know where he is, you'd better say so. Otherwise, you could be charged with wasting police time, which is an offence.'

He sounded pompous and official, like a policeman, Lisa told herself as she poured milk into the bowl. She pushed the cornflakes around with her spoon, concentrating on making the edges go soggy.

'I've told you, I don't know,' she said. 'But you don't believe me. I'm a suspect!'

'Don't be ridiculous!' snapped Mr McBride. 'Now look here, my girl — '

'George, leave it,' said Mum. She ruffled Lisa's hair. 'You didn't sleep much last night, did you? You're all puffs and shadows.'

Lisa did not answer. She simply put a spoonful of

cornflakes into her mouth and started to chew. The cornflakes tasted like small pieces of wet cardboard. There was a stony silence.

'Well, isn't this a jolly scene?' smiled Chris as he came into the dining room. 'You can just feel the good will and laughter bouncing off the walls.'

'That's enough, Chris,' said Mr McBride.

'Sorry, I'm sure.' Chris sat down and helped himself to cereal. 'Something wrong with your cornflakes, Sis? You don't seem to be enjoying them very much.'

Lisa flashed him an angry look. He smiled at her. 'Just growing pains, isn't it, Mum? We all have to go through it. Why, I remember my own first love. . . .'

'Oh, shut up!' Lisa pushed her chair back and jumped to her feet. 'I hate you!' she shouted, and ran up the stairs.

'Something I said?' murmured Chris, and tucked into his breakfast.

Lisa threw herself on the bed, but the tears seemed finally to have dried up. Fear and anger mixed together and set, like concrete, inside her. She would not give in. Tomorrow they would see Martin, and Martin would know what to do. Even if it meant owning up and getting into trouble, Martin would stand by them and stick up for them. He would talk to Mum and Dad, and the police. She just had to last until tomorrow.

Lisa wondered whether Fliss and Zeke, or Sally-Anne, had been questioned. She supposed they must have been, or at least would be this morning. What if one of them spilled it all? Fliss and Zeke would never talk, but Lisa was not sure about Sally-Anne, who was still a Junior, and more easily scared. Lisa decided she had to get the Gang together and find out exactly what was going on.

The bedroom door opened. It was Chris. He shut the door and sat down on the end of her bed.

'Go away,' said Lisa.

'I don't think you want me to, Sis,' he grinned.

'Go away,' she said again.

Chris leaned towards her, looking furtively all around him, as if he were a spy. Then he whispered, in a terrible foreign accent, 'I have information — important information!'

'What?' Lisa was startled.

'Mum and Dad have been talking about you. Wouldn't you like to know what they said?'

'No,' said Lisa stubbornly. 'I bet I know, anyway. Mum went on about growing up being so difficult for a young girl nowadays' — she mimicked her mother's voice, and Chris laughed — 'and Dad listened and then said they had to get to the bottom of all this.'

'Dead right!' said Chris. 'But there was more.' Chris looked straight at Lisa, his face unusually serious. 'Sis, just tell me. Do you know where Gary is?'

Lisa looked out of the window, her face set.

'I'm trying to help, Lisa, honestly. Look, you don't have to tell me everything, not if you don't want to, but just say yes or no — is Gary in that club hut of yours?'

Lisa whirled around. 'How did you. . .' she began, and then he stopped. 'You pig!'

'Now listen to me, Lisa. I'm not as close as Martin, and I don't want to be. But I am your big brother too, you know. Even if you are a real pain in the neck sometimes, family sticks together when there's trouble. And you're heading for plenty of that, if you're not careful. I will tell you something you really need to know, if you can promise me that Gary is safe and that he will go home on Saturday, just like his note says.'

Lisa looked at her brother carefully. Most of the time he could not be bothered with her, except to tease or crack a few daft jokes. Why did he want to help her now? She did not know whether to trust him or not. He certainly *looked* serious, not like he did when he was teasing her. Anyway, Chris had already guessed Gary was in the hut, hadn't he? Lisa nodded.

'He's safe,' she said quickly.

Chris went to the bedroom door and looked outside, then came back. 'Dad thinks you're lying,' he said in a low voice, 'but Mum thinks it's important to give you the benefit of the doubt. She says it's important not to accuse you if it turns out you're telling the truth. Dad also thinks Gary might be in the hut.'

Lisa's hand flew to her mouth. Chris nodded.

'Yes. They were talking about it in the kitchen, over the washing up, so I listened in,' said Chris shamelessly. 'Dad says, "Well, I'll have to go and look," and Mum says, "No. If he's not there, if she just happens to be telling the truth and you embarrass her in front of her friends, then we'll never get her to trust us again. And she won't tell us what's really troubling her." Anyway, they argued for a while and then decided what to do.'

Lisa watched him closely. 'Go on, then. What are they going to do?'

'Dad is going to have quiet word with the Tennesons,' Chris said. 'And when you all come in tonight, they're going to slip out and look in the hut. That way, if they're wrong, you kids need never know they were there. If they're right, the runaway is back home before nightfall. Crafty so-and-so. It's being so devious that makes him such a good cop, I suppose,' finished Chris.

He got up. 'That's it. You'd better find your true love somewhere else to hide, eh?'

With an effort, Lisa gave her brother a clumsy hug. 'Thanks, Chris.'

He shrugged. 'Any time. I've been to Gary's house, remember. I feel sorry for the poor kid. I'd probably run away too, if I was in his shoes.'

'Chris?'

'Yes?'

'Can you lend me a pound? I'll pay you back next week.

Chris tutted. 'I didn't charge you for the information, little sister,' he said. 'Thank your lucky stars for that.' With this, he left the room.

Lisa went downstairs slowly, ready to face another onslaught of questions. But Dad was just putting his jacket on.

'Where are you going?' asked Lisa nervously.

'Work,' he said. 'A new lead has just come up on the Thurlow Park robbery.'

'What's that?' asked Lisa, trying hard not to appear too interested.

'No time now – tell you later,' said Dad. He put his hand on her shoulder and kissed her cheek. ' 'Bye, lovely.' She knew he was trying to show her that he was not angry any more.

'Oh, Lisa – did you ask Dad for that pound?' said Mum suddenly.

'What pound? What do you want a pound for?'

'We're going on a picnic tomorrow,' said Lisa. 'The Gang, I mean.'

'You're *what*? Your best friend's gone missing, and you're off on a picnic? What's the matter with kids these days? Don't you worry about anything, at all?

68

I've heard it all now.' He was about to say more, but the telephone rang and he went into the hall to answer it. 'Yes, I have. No, I'll do that on my way in. Yes, I'm just leaving now.'

Mr McBride put down the phone and poked his head round the door. 'No, Lisa, you are not having a pound with which to celebrate the disappearance of your friend. Not from me – and not from your mum, either,' he said pointedly. He and his wife exchanged angry looks.

'You're causing trouble between Mum and Dad now,' she told herself, and miserably climbed the stairs.

On the dressing table in Lisa's room lay a one pound coin, and a scribbled note. 'You owe me a pound plus twenty pence interest – pay back by Sunday, or else!'

'Thanks, Chris,' whispered Lisa.

She ran down the stairs. 'Just going out!' she called to her mother, and was through the front door before Mrs McBride had time to answer. The heat hit her like a blast from an open fire as she stepped outside. It was already a hot day, with a sort of stuffy feel in the air.

Fliss and Zeke were in the hut with Gary. They all turned to Lisa eagerly as she whispered, 'Peter Pan's Pudding' through the keyhole and came in. They were supposed to change the password every day, but it had been forgotten in all the excitement.

'What's going on?' said Gary. 'Zeke says he saw my mum going to your house. Was she all right?'

Gary looked a bit grubby and his hair was sticking up at the back. He looked smaller, and sadder, than usual. Lisa could not tell him how frightened Mrs Harvey had been.

'She was scared of being outside the house,' said Lisa carefully. 'But Chris took her back, and she was all right. She doesn't know whether to believe the note or not, Gary. She's reported you missing to the police.'

'That's done it,' said Fliss quietly. 'They'll come searching, asking questions. They're bound to come here, aren't they?'

'If they don't, my dad will.' Lisa explained what Chris had told her. 'Where's Sally-Anne?' she asked. 'The police might get something out of her.'

'No problem today. She came first thing to bring her share of the money and tell us. Her gran's ill – had a fall or something, and Sal's mum had to go and look after her. Sal had to go too. They might not be back before tomorrow night, if the gran can't manage on her own.' Fliss frowned when she saw Lisa's relieved smile. 'But I think Sal can keep a secret just as well as any of us.'

Lisa changed the subject. 'We have to find somewhere else, just for tonight. Tomorrow it will all be over, one way or another.'

'I know just the place,' said Zeke. 'That is, if Gary wouldn't be scared to sleep in the woods tonight.'

' 'Course I wouldn't. I'm not scared of anything,' said Gary at once. Lisa looked at him admiringly, and he added, 'It's only dark, and dark can't hurt you. It's not like there are wolves or anything – are there?' he finished, looking as though he was not quite sure for a moment. But when Fliss and Zeke both laughed, as though he was cracking a good joke, Gary smiled again.

'Where in the woods, though?' asked Lisa. 'I know it's hot, but he can't just sleep on the ground, can he? Someone might decide to take a moonlit stroll, or something.' Lisa herself was terrified of being anywhere lonely in the dark. Whether Gary was scared or not, she did not like the idea of him being so far away from safety.

'I think there would be room in that little cavern we found by the stream,' said Zeke. 'It's only small, but so's Gary. He only needs room enough to lie down.'

They all looked at each other, considering the idea. Up in the woods, which started at the end of Wood Lane, was a small, fast-flowing stream. The Gang often played there, building dams and searching for gold. The place Zeke was talking about was not really a cave, more a large crack in the hilly bank above the stream. It went back a few feet into the hillside. They used it to store things when they were pretending to be gold-hunters, or outlaws. You had to paddle across the stream to reach it, and it always felt a bit damp.

'Will it be dry enough?' asked Lisa.

Zeke nodded. 'It hasn't rained for weeks,' he reminded her. 'And it's been so hot lately, that mud will be baked hard.'

'It will be awfully dark,' said Lisa doubtfully.

'I'll take a torch,' said Gary. 'I'm willing to give it a try. I can take some cushions from here, and a blanket just in case the floor is a bit damp. It will be a bit of an adventure.' Gary began to look a little more cheerful.

Lisa wondered if children ever died of heart attacks. Her stomach had begun churning all over again, and she had felt worried and anxious nearly every moment since she had agreed to go into Plymouth with Gary. If she worried much more, Lisa was sure she would not be able to survive it.

'Gary, let me tell my dad,' she said suddenly. 'You haven't done anything really wrong, I'm sure you haven't. Let me tell him. He'll be able to help us.

Anyway, it can't be worse than hiding away like this, and sleeping in the woods. It's . . . it's. . . .'

They were all looking at her in amazement. Lisa did not know why she was going against them, after letting it all get this far, but she had to carry on. 'It's so childish,' she said at last. 'We all expect Martin to know what to do, because he's grown-up and he's on our side. But I bet he'll just tell us to tell Dad anyway – we're going to look even more stupid than we do already.'

Lisa had not meant to sound snooty. She was surprised that the words came out that way, and wished she could have made it sound better, even if it was the truth.

'Stupid, are we?' said Zeke angrily. 'I suppose Gary's stupid to get away from his uncle, is he? I suppose it would be *clever* to just go home and get a belt on the other cheek – a matching pair, eh?'

Lisa had never seen Zeke really angry before. Fliss looked as though she couldn't believe Lisa had spoken at all.

'Lisa,' she said, 'If you've been thinking this all along, why say nothing until now? Have you been watching us, thinking how stupid we are, all this time?'

'No, of course not,' said Lisa, trying not to shout. Those awful tears, never far away, were pricking their way through to her cheeks again. 'But you must see. . . .'

'It doesn't matter,' said Gary bitterly. He stood up and went to peer out of the little window. His bruised side showed up clearly in the light coming through it. 'She'll tell anyway, won't she? When it comes down to it, she's a copper's kid.'

He could not have hurt her more, after all they had been through together, if he had hit her full in the face.

'That's not fair,' she said quietly. Then her anger took shape and she shouted at him. 'That's a snide, rotten thing to say. I can't help what my dad does for a living, but that doesn't matter to you lot; you've held it against me right from the start. Do you really think my dad has nothing better to do than snoop around after a bunch of kids? He couldn't care less, but that doesn't stop you getting at me, does it? Copper's kid, is it? Well, if you think I care more about keeping out of trouble than snitching on my friends, there's no more to be said, is there?'

Lisa stalked to the door, and no one spoke or tried to stop her. She opened the door and turned. Her voice wobbled a bit, but it was as cold as ice.

'You hide in the woods, Gary Harvey. Don't you worry, I won't tell.' Lisa looked at them all, straight in the eyes, one by one. 'I wouldn't waste my time,' she said, and walked across the garden with her head held high.

Lisa wondered what they would do now. They could not go and see Martin without her – Lisa had the address, and knew the way. For a moment, her step slowed. Perhaps she should go back and give it to them, at least? Then she remembered the three accusing faces. 'Copper's kid': it was 'Good old Lisa' when she could be useful to them, and 'Copper's kid' when she disagreed. No, let them sort it out on their own. That would show them.

Mum and Dad were both out when Lisa arrived home. Chris looked up in surprise from the newspaper as his little sister flung open the door and strode into the kitchen, her face dark with anger.

'Trouble?' he said.

'I'm fed up with that stupid Gang, that's all.'

'Why, what have they done?'

Lisa hesitated. She badly wanted to tell Chris everything. Had he ever been called 'copper's kid'? It had never seemed to worry him. She just did not know whether Chris, who called her a pain and teased her most of the time, could be trusted as much as Martin. It would depend on his mood at the time, and that was too risky. If the secret came out, it would only prove the others right.

'They're just children,' she said, 'playing silly games.'

'I do declare, Sis. You're beginning to grow up,' laughed Chris.

'You sound just like Mum.' Lisa threw a soggy tea towel half-heartedly at her brother and wandered into the dining room. For some time she stared out of the open window, opening it wide and moving it like a fan, trying to make a breeze. There was a stillness in the hot streets outside which was almost suffocating; there seemed to be no movement in the air at all.

Something at the end of Elderberry Walk caught Lisa's eye. Old Fogarty was coming to wash his car, as he always did on a Thursday afternoon. 'All spruce and ship-shape for the weekend,' he had said to Lisa once, in one of his rare friendly moments. Lisa pressed her cheek against the cool glass and watched him as he worked.

Fliss and Zeke came down their drive, wheeling their bikes. They went out of their gate. Fliss turned up the alley, but Zeke stood for a moment. Lisa sat up straight. They were going through with it, then. Gary would be nipping over the garden wall into the alley further up, once Fliss and Zeke had given the all-clear from each end. He would have to share Zeke's bike. It would make more sense for him to borrow Lisa's. Suddenly, Lisa ached to be a part of it all again.

Zeke looked at Old Fogarty, who was lovingly spreading the suds over his little wite car. Then Zeke looked carefully up and down Elderberry Walk, finally catching Lisa's eye. She drew back from the window, but Zeke had beckoned to her. Lisa sat down at the dining table and fingered a place mat. Why should she go? She was not part of the Gang any more, and she was certainly not at the beck and call of its leader. Nonetheless, a moment later Lisa was reluctantly opening the front door and walking steadily across the road. Perhaps they were all feeling sorry now.

'We're going to do it,' said Zeke in a low voice. 'I'm going to go with Gary to Exeter.'

'You don't know where to go,' said Lisa, preparing for her chance to get back into the adventure. Zeke only had to ask, to hint, even, and Lisa would see it through whatever happened.

'We know he's in the University,' said Zeke. 'If you won't give us the address, we'll ask the porters or something. We'll find him, somehow. But Lisa – you won't tell, will you? Promise?'

This was no apology. They had already worked out what to do without Lisa. Not only that, they thought she would refuse to give them any help at all. And Zeke still didn't quite trust her. Lisa felt as though a door she had been about to pass through had been deliberately slammed on her.

'Go to the porters' lodge,' she said. 'Ask them to show you D staircase. Room 102.' She turned on her heel and looked angrily over her shoulder as she walked away.

'Lisa! Lisa, come here a minute,' she heard Zeke call.

But she would not turn back. By the time Lisa had gone into the house and looked out of the dining-room window, Zeke was gone.

They were going ahead without her.

Nine

After leaving Zeke at the bottom of the alley, Lisa stayed in her own back garden, stretched out flat in the sun with a book to read. The grass tickled her bare legs, and occasionally she could feel an insect crawling across her arm. At least the sun was warm on her back, and you could just about breathe in the garden. Even with all the windows open the house still felt closed-up, like a tomb.

Lisa kept thinking about Gary, in the dark, mud-baked cavern. It must be horrible. Perhaps the others would stay with him until teatime. They would paddle in the stream, build another dam, or search for early blackberries.

Lisa sighed and turned back to the book. It was an interesting story, but she found it difficult to concentrate. The sun, and the lack of any cooling breeze, made her feel tired all afternoon. Mum had prepared a crispy salad for dinner, with bread rolls and ice cream from the freezer. It was as much as anyone could face in this weather. Even chewing is a big effort when you are exhausted.

By the time Mum coughed and looked pointedly at the clock, which was the signal for bedtime, Lisa could hardly keep her eyes open. She had not slept very well at all for the past two nights. Although she dreaded the moment when she turned out the bedside lamp and pulled the sheet over her, ready for sleep, Lisa did not see the flannel man tonight. Before she could even properly picture Gary, alone and probably a bit scared in the darkness, Lisa was asleep. She did not dream at all.

The crash that woke her was so loud, and so near, Lisa was up and out of bed, ready to run, before she even knew she was awake. The room felt cooler. Her curtains billowed in a breeze which came through the open window. The crash had been a bolt of thunder. It was raining, and raining very hard. Lisa watched the great, heavy drops pounding the window-sill with growing horror. Some landed inside, on top of her collection of china animals. They looked as though they were off for a paddle along the window shelf.

Suddenly the sky lit up with a vivid orange-yellow streak, forking in two at the bottom. Almost at the same time came another colossal clap of thunder, and the rain drove even harder against the sill.

'Dead above us!' whispered Lisa.

It was a real West Country storm at its worst, throwing itself in from the sea like a battering ram, battling right over the houses in Elderberry Walk. Within seconds, it could overflow drains, knock fruit from trees and flood gardens and cellars. Rivers and streams would rise, bursting their banks. . . .

'Gary!'

Lisa pulled on the shorts and T-shirt she had left on the floor, tucking her flimsy nightdress clumsily into the shorts. The stream up in the woods would certainly have risen and flooded the little cave. It was unlikely that Gary would have slept through the start of the storm, but he would have been very tired after all that had happened. Lisa had to make sure that he was all right.

'Lisa — Lisa, are you awake?' It was her mother, knocking at the door. Lisa sprang to open it, before she could come in and discover Lisa dressed to go out in the middle of the night, with a raging storm outside. Opening the door just a crack, Lisa showed her face.

'I'm fine, Mum. I'm not scared. It's quite a storm, isn't it?'

'It certainly is. Make sure your windows are closed, or you'll be swimming down to breakfast tomorrow. Good night.'

' 'Night, Mum.' Lisa shut the door and dived into the clutter at the bottom of the wardrobe. Her hand closed around the box of chocolates Gary had given her; she pushed it impatiently aside. Wellingtons and a mac were in there somewhere, shoved further and further back as the weather had continued to hold through the summer holidays.

It seemed ages before Lisa found them, but she was finally ready and tiptoed out of the room. Another crash of thunder just as she reached the top of the stairs nearly made her call out, but she carried on and reached the back door without alerting anyone in the house.

In all this time, Lisa had only one thought — to find Gary and make sure he was safe. It was only as she turned the handle of the door which would take her into the garage where her bike was stored that Lisa realized she was absolutely terrified. Not just scared, like you were when a teacher wanted to see you after the lesson or the dentist said you had to have a filling. This was something different altogether. Her feet did not want to move.

The rain banged against the door outside. Lisa peeped through the kitchen window. It was completely dark. Even the street lamps were out. She would need a torch.

'Come on,' she said to herself. 'It's only dark. Just an absence of light, a nothingness. And *nothing* can't harm you, can it?'

With a sudden short burst of courage, Lisa was out of the kitchen door and into the garage. She flicked on the light switch and got the torch down from its hook on the wall. Carefully, she checked its beam, and then checked the lights on her bike. She would have to man-handle the bike through the kitchen door; the garage doors made too much noise, even above the rain.

Lisa wheeled the bike into the kitchen and slowly drew back the bolt on the door. She was ready. After all, the dark outside was the same dark that filled her bedroom every night. It could do her no harm.

'It's no darker out there than in your bedroom,' she told herself as her hand hesitated on the handle. But still she could not open the door. The dark in Lisa's bedroom was different. It was a friendly dark. Lisa knew it well. She knew the half-shadows, the outlines of the furniture caught in the moonbeams. Besides, her bedside light was always just an arm-stretch away.

The dark outside was unknown, unfriendly. Lisa was afraid of it. Gary must be afraid by now, too.

'Lisa McBride, don't be silly,' she said aloud in her best 'teacher' voice. 'Now, get out there and get on with it!'

She pushed open the door and struggled to pick up the bike and lift it over the step and into the garden. The door swung behind her – Lisa was only just in time to stop it crashing shut. The sky lit up again, but this time it was a few seconds before the thunder. The storm was moving away.

The rain soaked Lisa almost as soon as she stepped outside. She had forgotten to button the mac, and her

T-shirt and nightdress stuck to her. Lisa fumbled for the buttons, although she did not honestly believe she could get any more wet than she was. The torch jumped up and down in the basket as Lisa set off down the drive. She hoped Mum and Dad, whose bedroom was at the front, would not be looking out.

The street was darker than Lisa had ever known it. The rain made it impossible to see further than a few feet ahead. As she reached the alleyway, Lisa looked up at the Tennesons' house. It occurred to her, for the first time, that Fliss and Zeke had probably been woken by the storm as well. In the hall window upstairs a dim light burned; it was the one they always left on at night. There were no other signs of life, but Fliss and Zeke both had their bedrooms at the back of the house, so Lisa couldn't tell if they were awake.

Lisa hesitated yet again by the alley, wiping the rain-water from her face. The rain was going right through her clothes. Even her skin was wet underneath it all. The alley was very dark, with the lamp out. The woods would be even blacker. Lisa did not know for *sure* that Gary was in the cavern. Perhaps they had changed their minds. She would look a right fool if she went crashing off to look for a boy who right at this moment was tucked up in his warm bed. Lisa knew this was really unlikely. Still, she was not a part of it any more, was she? Why should she do anything? Fliss and Zeke were in charge. Let them handle it.

For one moment, Lisa almost convinced herself. She even turned her bike round and took a couple of steps towards her own house, and safety. Then she imagined Gary, trapped and calling for help. No one would hear him, only the trees and the animals of the night. What if Fliss and Zeke had somehow slept through the storm?

Or could not get out of the house without being seen, and stopped? Lisa had to go; she had to be sure.

Quickly Lisa got on to her bike and rode up the alley, shivering with cold and fright. It was a steep hill, and she had to force her knees to push down the pedals. At the top of the alley she turned left. A few of the houses had lights on, but at the end of Wood Lane there were no more houses. On the other side of the road which ran across Wood Lane at the top, the woods began.

Lisa left her bike propped up against the fence on the edge of the woods and set off. The rough path was slippery with wet mud, although there were drier patches where the thick trees overhead had shielded the path from the worst of the rain. There was no sound except for water; Lisa could hear the stream off to her right. She had to point the torch at the ground because she could hardly see anything. 'No one knows you're here,' said the voice inside her. 'No one will come looking for you.'

Suddenly Lisa became convinced someone was following her. Quickly she turned around, swinging the torch in a wide arc. The beam picked out tree trunks as it swung, making them look almost liquid and very sinister. They did not look at all like the trees she so often climbed in and camped beneath. There was no one there, only the wind. The trees swayed restlessly, moving their branches towards each other as if they were talking about her. Silly Lisa, out all alone in the night, they seemed to say. Anything could happen, they moaned, anything. A sob rose up inside her, echoed by the wind through the trees. She moved on faster, sliding on the mud.

The stream was a little way off the path, further up. When Lisa reached the old fallen tree which they used as a lookout post, she knew she was almost there. The cave was just about in line with the trunk. Lisa could not see the stream, even with the torch, but she could hear the rush of water. The rain had almost stopped, and there was only a steady drip from the tall trees surrounding her.

Lisa put her back against the tree trunk, right in the middle. That way she could move a little to the right or the left without losing the cavern. She moved off, keeping her feet in as straight a line as she could through the thick, wet foliage. It was about fifty paces, she thought. After forty-eight, Lisa saw the stream. It looked awfully high, but perhaps that was just her imagination.

Lisa had stopped a few paces away from the bank. The stream was quite a bit higher than her boots, she judged. Lisa flashed the torch onto the other side of the stream.

The cave was not there. There was a lot of churned-up mud, with pieces of tree root poking out from it, but no cave. Lisa felt her stomach give a sickening lurch.

'Gary! Gary!' she shouted, waving the torch. Her voice sounded muffled. Keep calm, she told herself sternly. You must have gone too far from a straight line. Keep calm, go back to the path, and start again.

Lisa was shivering so much now that she could hardly move. She walked back the way she had come, again trying to keep a straight path. After forty-seven paces she hit the tree trunk. There had been no mistake. Lisa turned round and walked back again. She ended up in exactly the same spot.

'Gary!' she screamed, her voice not sounding like a girl's voice at all. 'Gary, where are you? Gary – answer me. Oh please, please answer me. . . .'

The rainwater dripped steadily off the trees, the stream rushed on with no thought for the terrified child standing beside it. Lisa realized now what had happened. The cave, which had never been a proper cave in the first place, had been filled below from the stream, and the mud roof had caved in. That mass of mud which dipped away from the rest of the bank had been Gary's hiding place. Now it looked as though it would be his grave.

Gary must be underneath the mud. Lisa, who was sobbing and screaming in turn, waded into the stream and beat her fists on the mound of mud. Some of it slipped into the water and sank to the bottom. Lisa tried not to give in to the panic which had made her enter the water without knowing what she was doing. She could not do anything – even if Gary was still, somehow, alive, Lisa could not dig him out with her bare hands. She climbed out of the stream and stood for a few seconds, hoping against hope that she would hear Gary's voice: 'I'm all right, Lisa. Here – over here!' But the only sound was the rushing water.

Lisa turned away and ran, slipping and sliding, her feet awash inside the wellingtons. Slipping, sliding, falling over and over again until she was covered in mud and leaves, Lisa almost missed the path entirely. She had to force herself to go a little more slowly. It seemed hours before she reached her bike, and when she got onto it, the pedals would not turn fast enough.

Instead of freewheeling down the steep alleyway, Lisa kept pedalling, and hurtled into Elderberry Walk like a bullet. Throwing her bike down by the back door, Lisa flung it open and ran up the stairs. A trail of mud and water followed her.

Mr and Mrs McBride were fast asleep when the door burst open. Mr McBride sat bolt upright, swearing.

'What the – !' He stared at Lisa.

His wife sat up groggily beside him. 'Lisa!'

Their daughter, whom they had imagined was snuggled down in her cosy bed, was standing beside them covered in mud. Her hair was plastered to her head, and filthy water dripped from her clothes to form muddy pools on the beige carpet. She was sobbing and talking at the same time. They could make no sense of it at all.

'Lisa, what is it? Slow down; tell me what's the matter.' Her father started to climb out of bed.

The room started to whirl about her. Lisa thought she was going to fall, and felt an arm around her shoulder; Chris had come in behind her.

'Oh, Dad,' she blubbered. 'Gary's dead – and it's all my fault!'

Ten

It took Detective Inspector McBride less than a minute to extract the information he needed from Lisa. He waved aside her attempts to explain more with a short, 'Later!'

'Chris, get more torches, rope, and a couple of blankets. You should find it all under the stairs.' He turned to his wife. 'Jill, you'd better call the local station. See if they can send a couple of men. Call the fire brigade and the ambulance as well. We'll meet them there — main path, hundred yards or so up. I'll leave Lisa with a torch to show where to leave the main path.'

'George, you can't take Lisa. Look at her! She's had enough for one night.'

Lisa opened her mouth to protest, but when Dad looked at her she shut it again.

'It's about time she learned what the real world is all about,' he said. 'She and her friends started all this; she can see it through to the end. Come on, Lisa.'

Miserably, Lisa followed her father downstairs and waited by the front door while he backed the car out of the garage. She was relieved he was not going to leave her behind, but he was clearly very angry. Her heart sank at the thought of police and firemen, and the ambulance, all dashing to the scene, and all demanding to know how on earth a boy came to be in the woods at that time of night in the first place.

'Oh, please,' she whispered. 'Please, just let him be all right. I'll take all the blame; I'll take *twice* the blame. I'll even go to prison. Only, just let him be all right.'

Quite who Lisa was making this wild bargain with, she did not know. It comforted her a little bit, but Chris and Dad's icy silence as they drove down Elderberry Walk, with Lisa sitting meekly on the back seat, took even that comfort away.

'I'm sorry, Dad,' she said.

'I'll bet,' was his only answer. It made her feel cold inside.

'Don't worry, Sis. He'll be all right.' Chris took pity on her. He turned and smiled. His face was white and his mouth looked tight. Lisa knew he did not really believe what he was saying.

When they reached the woods, Dad pulled the car off the road and they unloaded the rope and blankets. The rain had almost stopped now, and the thunder could barely be heard in the distance. With a torch each, the path was more visible, and the three of them made quicker progress than Lisa had been able to on her own. When they reached the fallen tree, Lisa explained how she had found the spot where the hide-out should be.

'Right,' said Dad. 'Keep the torch on – the emergency services should be here soon, and you'll need to show the way. OK, Chris?'

Chris nodded and they set off. The rain could not be felt here, under the trees, just the steady drip of collected rainwater on the leaves. Lisa, left alone on the main path, could hear movement all around her as animals and insects came out to take stock of their surroundings after the storm. What would they make of her?

Lisa wondered whether snakes liked the rain. She

could not remember whether they were likely to come out at night or not. She stamped her feet up and down, moving on the spot to frighten away any creatures that might want to investigate this new addition to their night-time territory. Then it occurred to her that *something* might mistake her for a rabbit, or some other sort of food, and attack. She stood absolutely still, but as soon as she did this, she felt sure something was crawling over her feet. In the end she decided to compromise, and stood still except for her torch, which she swung around her feet, checking the ground very carefully.

There was no sound from Chris or Dad, although they were not so far away. Perhaps something had happened to them. Lisa shone her torch towards the stream. The beam ended in black nothingness. 'Oh please, let him be all right,' Lisa said. 'I'll do anything. . . .' and she made some more wild bargains.

Perhaps Gary was not even there. He could have gone home, owned up, gone back to the hut. That would explain why Fliss and Zeke were not here. Surely they would be as anxious as Lisa. They might have got here earlier, and taken Gary back with them. Lisa would look a proper fool, with all these men working through the night for nothing. Dad would be so cross he might never forgive her. Lisa found herself hoping Gary *was* in the cave; not seriously hurt, of course, just injured enough to make it worthwhile calling an ambulance. Almost at once she felt very ashamed of these thoughts, and went back to making promises about what she would do, if only Gary were safe.

A powerful beam of light caught her and she looked impatiently down the path. 'Over here!' she called. 'Hurry!'

At first, Lisa could see only a round, dazzling light

and then the faint outline of a peaked cap. As the light drew nearer, Lisa could make out several dark forms with pink, shapeless blobs where faces should be. It was the police and rescue service. They arrived together, two uniformed constables and three firemen, carrying some heavy-looking machinery.

'Where is he, sweetheart?' one of the firemen asked kindly.

Lisa pointed. Then, 'I'll come and show you,' she said.

'No!' said the fireman sharply. He saw Lisa's white face tighten and said more gently, 'best not, eh? We don't know what we'll find. Best you stay here. You keep that torch pointing along the path, there's a love. Then we'll be able to find our way back, won't we? And the ambulance isn't here yet.'

He patted her shoulder and then the five men set off together. They made a good deal more noise than Chris and Dad had done, and Lisa could follow their progress. There was a spluttering, coughing sound, a bit like Chris's moped when he started it up, and then the steady thump of some sort of engine. Lisa strained her eyes. She could see that a very bright lamp arrangement had been rigged up, and moving pinpoints of light which must be the men moving around with their torches. Shadowy shapes moved in and out of the arc of light which fell from the fixed beam lanterns. She could not see what they were doing. They must have some sort of mechanical digger.

Lisa could feel her legs beginning to give way. She climbed onto the end of the fallen tree trunk, watching the distant lights. Dad had left one of the blankets with her. Lisa wrapped it around her shoulders and tried to huddle inside it and still keep her balance on the knobbly trunk. She felt very cold.

Just last week, Lisa had longed to feel cold. Summer had gone on for so long, and the heat was so tiring, she would have welcomed a snowstorm, even.

Her wet clothes made her shiver. 'Well, you got what you wanted, my girl,' she could almost hear Dad saying.

Suddenly the beat of the machine stopped. The pinpoints were still, and then they all moved towards one place. They had found him. Lisa clambered off the trunk. The lights were bobbing about, but none of them moved towards her.

'We don't know what we'll find.' The fireman's voice echoed in Lisa's head. He was being kind, that was it. He did not think there was much hope of finding Gary alive, and he did not want Lisa to be around when Gary's mangled body was pulled from the cave.

Throwing aside the blanket, Lisa slipped and slid through the undergrowth towards the lights. As soon as she could see the dark shape of a fireman, she called out, 'Have you got him? Is he . . . is he . . .' she could not bring herself to ask if he was still alive.

Lisa reached the bank, and Dad's hand gripped her arm, or she would have slipped over and into the water.

'Where is he?' shouted Lisa. 'What's happened?' She was almost hysterical. Why was no one saying anything? A policeman was talking into his radio. The other policemen and a fireman were rolling up a hose. No one was taking any notice of Lisa.

'Hello, Lisa.' It was Gary's voice.

Lisa turned, unbelieving. There sat Gary, wrapped in a blanket, perched on top of the machinery. He gave her a weak smile.

'I'm all right,' he said in a wobbly voice. The biggest

fireman lifted him up and started off towards the path. Gary, fierce and independent Gary, did not utter a single word of protest. He clung to the fireman, leaning his head on the fireman's shoulder like an exhausted infant. He allowed himself to be carried like a baby back to the edge of the woods, and the blue flashing lights of the emergency vehicles.

An ambulance had drawn up and was waiting with its doors open. Gary was bundled inside. He turned a terrified face towards Lisa, standing outside with her father. The cold whiteness of the ambulance above the red blankets made Gary look like a very small, lost animal, swamped in a laboratory. He was absolutely filthy. It would be difficult to tell what colour he was, or even if he was a boy or a girl. As the doors closed, Lisa saw an ambulanceman move towards him with another blanket.

'Does he have to go to hospital?' she asked her dad. 'He hates hospitals; he told me once. I suppose it's because his dad died in one. Is he badly hurt, Dad? Will he be all right? How did you get him free? I thought he was . . . oh, Dad!' Lisa wailed, and buried her head in the thick, wet coat.

'He'll be fine, love. He's shocked, that's all. He wasn't in that cavern you described, you know. Just as well – he wouldn't have stood a chance.'

'Not there?' Lisa drew away in astonishment and looked up at her father. 'Where was he, then?'

'Apparently, he got out as soon as the storm started. He moved further back, into the woods. When the storm really got going he crawled into some bracken and under some bushes. He's badly frightened, very wet and cold of course, but there are no bones broken. They'll give him a good look-over at the hospital – and

91

a bath, I shouldn't wonder – and he'll be home by morning with any luck.'

The mention of the hospital giving Gary a thorough examination made Lisa remember the bruises on his body. Would they be able to tell where they had come from? If not, and if Gary wouldn't tell, who knew what could happen when he returned home?

'Dad,' she said, 'I think his uncle will really hurt him if he goes home.'

McBride looked at her sharply. 'More secrets, eh, Lisa? Don't you worry about Gary. I think you'll find Chris and your mother already have their fingers stuck into that pie.'

Lisa did not understand what he meant, but she was too tired to ask for an explanation. She leaned back against Dad. 'He didn't answer when I called,' she said, almost dreamily. 'He didn't make a sound.'

'I expect he didn't hear you. He was quite far away. He heard the noise of the digger, saw the lights, and made his way over to us.'

'He gave himself up, then,' said Lisa. That made her feel a lot better. Lisa knew she could have done nothing differently, but it had occurred to her that if Gary was not trapped in the cavern and Lisa called out a search party, he would feel betrayed.

'I'd better go and sort this out,' said Dad, indicating the little group of police and firemen who had watched the ambulance pull off and were now standing together, having reloaded the fire engine with its rescue equipment. 'Stay with Lisa, Chris.'

Chris put his arm tightly around Lisa's shoulder as Dad pushed her gently over to her brother. They watched Dad talking to the constables. The men nodded respectfully, and got into their car. The firemen had a few words with Dad as well, and they looked over to Lisa. She wondered what they were saying. Then they climbed up into the engine and rode off after the police car. The night was beginning to fade, and the blackness that had surrounded them was turning into murky grey.

The three McBrides stood quietly together by the dark outline of their car. It had been quite a night. For a while none of them spoke, watching the tail lights of the fire engine moving further and further away, until they could see nothing but the dark grey sky on the black road.

'Come on,' said Dad. 'Your mum will be worried stiff. Let's go home.'

Eleven

Mum was waiting in the warm, brightly-lit kitchen. Dad answered her questioning look with a smile and an upraised thumb.

'Oh, thank God,' said Mum, and hugged Lisa until she thought she would have to cry out or be squeezed to death. There was mud all over her fleecy blue dressing gown when Mum finally let go of Lisa, but she did not seem to notice.

'Upstairs and into the bath, Lisa. You're filthy, and wet through. I've put the immersion heater on, so there should be plenty of hot water for Chris and your dad as well. I'll make some cocoa – we could all do with a hot drink.'

Lisa turned to her father. She had never thought of him as old, but she felt a sudden pang of fear as she saw wrinkles and lines she had never noticed before. Lisa had always seen him as the young, strong giant who lifted her onto his shoulders and swung her up into the air. But that was a picture from years ago, when Lisa was a little girl. Dad looked old, and tired. Lisa wondered what was going though his mind. He must be very disappointed in his daughter.

'I'm sorry, Dad,' she said for the second time. She knew it was a useless thing to say, but could think of nothing else.

'I know,' he said. He was not cross this time, and he

smiled at her quite gently. 'Go on, get cleaned up. Then you can tell us all about it, right from the beginning.' He gave her a shove towards the door. As Lisa went up the stairs she heard Dad say something, and Mum and Chris laughed. The tension was gone. It would not be easy to explain how Gary came to be in the woods tonight, but at least it was all out in the open, come what may. Lisa was not going to tell any more lies. It was like being in sinking sand: the more you struggled, lying to get out of trouble, the further in you went.

Lisa sank back into the steamy bath and watched her old rubber duck bobbing slowly up and down on the water. There was no sound. The rushing stream, the menacing trees, the rain and the mud and the terrifying darkness, were all still there. But they were outside, with the door firmly closed against them, and Mum and Dad between Lisa and danger. Lisa was here, in the sunshine-yellow bathroom, warm and safe. She would not have to go back.

The rubber duck tipped onto its nose as Lisa nudged it with her toe. She began to laugh, and could not stop. It was so funny, to be here playing with a rubber duck when she had almost had to face up to death in the woods. The more Lisa thought about it, the funnier it seemed, and Lisa could hardly dry herself for giggling. She twisted her clean pyjamas into an impossible tangle, and that made things worse. She went into the kitchen with tears streaming down her face, she had laughed so much.

'That old rubber duck,' she said, 'looks so ridiculous —' but now, all at once, Lisa did not find it funny at all, and she sobbed as Dad pulled her onto his lap.

'Shock,' he said. 'Just cry it out. You're safe now, both of you.'

Some minutes later, Lisa blew her nose and sat up. She moved off Dad's lap and went to sit on one of the hard kitchen chairs. Mum, Chris and Dad were all looking at her expectantly. Lisa took a deep breath, and began. She told them all about the medal, and about going into Plymouth with Gary. Dad sat forward, listening intently, and he nodded at Mum when Lisa got to the bit about Gary's bruised face.

'I thought it was unlikely he had got that in the woods,' he said.

Lisa did not tell him about the other bruises. That was up to Gary. As she went on with her story, Mum shook her head gently. Chris just gaped in astonishment.

'You great idiot!' Chris said, when she had finished. 'Why didn't you tell one of us at the start? What did you think the police were going to do, for heaven's sake? Clap you all in irons, just because a kid found something and sold it?'

'We didn't know,' said Lisa indignantly. 'In any case, I did want to tell, in the end. But it wasn't my secret. I couldn't snitch on Gary. It would have been all over, with the Gang, I mean, if I'd done that.'

'The Gang,' sneered Chris. 'A right bunch of twits you all turned out to be when you put your heads together. That kid could have been really badly hurt, even killed.'

'I think she knows that, Chris,' said Mum.

There was silence. Dad reached into his pocket for his pipe.

'What will happen now?' asked Lisa.

Dad shrugged. 'Nothing, until tomorrow,' he said. 'We'll wait and see how the boy is, first.'

Mum opened her mouth to say something, but Dad said quickly, 'Now, that's enough talking. You get to bed and get some sleep.'

'I couldn't,' said Lisa. 'My body wants to, but my head is just racing round and round.'

All the same, once she was in bed, Lisa could not keep her eyes open. When she woke up the sun was shining full into her bedroom, and it was very warm. The clock by the bed said twenty past twelve. Lisa shot out of bed and threw on some clothes.

Dad was on the telephone in the hall. He watched Lisa come down the stairs. 'She's just up,' he said, 'I'll bring them all in myelf — about half an hour? Fine. 'Bye.'

'Bring who in?' asked Lisa nervously. 'What's happening?'

'We're going to the police station,' said Dad. 'The Tennesons, you, me and Gary. . . .'

'Is he all right?'

Dad nodded. 'He's back home, for the moment.'

'Will we be arrested?' asked Lisa in a very small voice.

Dad laughed. 'No. You deserve to be, I'll grant you, but we have to save the room in our top security jails for slightly more hardened criminals. You'll have to tell the inspector what happened, that's all. I dare say he'll have a few things to say to you, as well.'

The journey to the police station was a miserable one. Gary and Lisa sat in the back of Dad's car in silence, wondering what was going to happen. Behind them was the Tennesons' car, with the whole family in it. Mrs Harvey had refused to come, saying she was too unwell, and the uncle was nowhere to be seen. So Mum had agreed to be responsible for Gary, 'in loco parentis', as she put it. Lisa did not understand why this should be necessary. She felt it would be best not to ask questions though. Mum was not being Mum today. She was wearing a suit, the suit she wore when she went to court with her clients – a brisk, efficient Social Worker. Lisa did not feel able to talk to her.

Lisa was surprised to see Sally-Anne at the police station when they arrived, with both her parents. Sally-Anne's dad had obviously taken the day off work, and looked most uncomfortable in his best dark woollen suit. It was blazing hot outside. They all looked very strained, and Sally-Anne had clearly been crying.

After a long, nerve-racking time, everyone was shepherded into a big bare room by a policeman in shirt sleeves. There were chairs against one wall and a table in the middle of the room. The parents all sat down and the children were told to stand in a line in front of the table. Then a big, stern man in an inspector's uniform came in, carrying a large book which he slammed down on the table. They all jumped, and Sally-Anne started to cry quietly.

Slowly, they all gave their versions of what had happened, and the part each child had played. A constable wrote down every single word they said, and it made them all very nervous. At the end, the parents had to sign everything that had been said. The papers were clipped together, and the constable left the room. A policewoman stood quietly in the corner, not looking at them.

Lisa exchanged a brief smile with Fliss, but no sooner had they begun to relax than the inspector started shouting at them. He told them all, in no uncertain terms, exactly what he thought of their behaviour. Even Zeke was close to tears by the time he had finished. Gary and Fliss stared at the floor, Sally sobbed, and Lisa looked steadily out of the window, her face the reddest it had ever been.

'Now, I've spoken to your parents,' the inspector was saying. 'They assure me nothing like this is ever going to happen again.'

He looked questioningly at Mr Tenneson, who cleared his throat and said, 'Certainly not. I'll have the key to the hut, Zeke – it's out of bounds at least until after Christmas. After that, well, it's up to you to prove you can be trusted to be out of our sight.'

'But that's months!' said Zeke, horrified.

'Then learn the lesson, lad, so it needn't happen again,' said the inspector. 'You're very lucky we're prepared to let it go at that. You've hampered a robbery investigation, withheld information, risked the safety of police, firemen, ambulancemen – to say nothing of the people who could have been left without emergency services last night through no fault of their own. While these men were out searching for young Mr Harvey here, someone who really needed help could have died. It was only luck that this didn't happen.

'Now, I've got a note of your names, and I'm going to remember them. And let me hear just one whiff of a rumour that any one of these names is involved in trouble again, and I'll be round your house. Just you make sure I never have cause to meet you in this police station again. Right – clear off.'

Thoroughly subdued, the Gang filed out of the room. Sally-Anne was quickly led away by her parents, whose expressions clearly showed that they believed their daughter had been led astray by the older ones.

'They're right, I suppose,' thought Lisa. 'We should have known better.'

They all piled back into the cars and drove home. As they turned into Elderberry Walk, Old Fogarty was washing his car. This was very strange. It was Friday today, and Friday was the day he took Mrs Fogarty shopping, in Plymouth. Fogarty never changed his routine, and surely he had washed his car yesterday – yes, Lisa remembered seeing him when she went to speak to Zeke at the bottom of the aley.

'Mr Fogarty must have seen us all leave,' said Dad with a chuckle.

Mum smiled. 'Wouldn't he just love to know where we've been?' she said over her shoulder. Lisa and Gary exchanged nervous grins. They would never hear the last of this from Old Fogarty.

The Tennesons had invited everyone in for some lunch. As they all stood in the drive Mr Fogarty straightened up and came over to the low wall that separated the two front gardens, his sponge dripping in his hand.

'Been somewhere nice?' he asked conversationally.

'Not lately,' said Dad. 'How about you?'

Old Fogarty looked confused. 'No. Er – no. Just washing the car.'

'And very smart it looks, too,' said Dad. 'Even better than it looked yesterday.'

For a moment Old Fogarty was at a loss, but he soon recovered himself. 'Hmm, well, that gleaming Mercedes the other day put my old car to shame.'

'What Mercedes?' asked Mrs Tenneson politely, since this was clearly what Fogarty was waiting for.

'You mean, you didn't see it?'

Old Fogarty was in his element now. He believed himself to be the foremost authority on everything that happened in Elderberry Walk, however small. 'It was a beautiful car – not brand new, mind, but not a scratch on her. That polish caught the lamplight like a mirror. She sparkled, did that car. Two men inside just sat there, outside your gate. Naturally, I thought they had called on you, found you out, and decided to wait; although I must say I hadn't seen anyone leaving the house,' he added almost accusingly.

Lisa tried not to laugh. Old Fogarty was quite puzzled at the thought that someone might have escaped from Elderberry Walk without his noticing. He would make a good prison guard.

'Well,' continued Fogarty, 'I had to go and help the wife with something, and I forgot about them. Next time I just happened to pass by the window, they were gone. Came back next day, mind, and walked up the alley. They weren't visiting you, then?'

Mrs Tenneson looked puzzled. 'No. One or other of us has been home all week, anyway, so they can't have been looking for us.'

'Tuesday night, it was,' said Old Fogarty. 'And again on Wednesday morning.'

Lisa, who could not pretend to be interested in a car containing people she did not even know, shuffled her feet. Fogarty was a boring old fool. She started to edge towards the house, but Dad suddenly snapped into a state of quiet excitement.

'Tuesday night?' he said. 'Jill, I'll bet any money it was the getaway car!'

'Of course,' breathed Mrs McBride. 'And back here on Wednesday, when they realized they'd dropped something, to try and cover their tracks.'

'By which time Gary had already found our first clue,' finished George McBride.

'Clue?' Old Fogarty's eyes were almost popping out of his head. 'Something important, eh? Always glad to help, Detective Inspector McBride, you know that.'

'You've been a great help already, Mr Fogarty,' said Dad. 'I may well be back to talk to you again in a minute or two.' He turned to the Tennesons. 'Look, I'd better get home and telephone the station. We'll need to follow this up at once. Will you excuse me?'

'Of course, George,' said Mrs Tenneson. 'Join us later, if you can. Cheerio.'

The children entered the house in a state of great excitement.

'Well, Dad,' said Zeke gleefully. 'Looks like it was a good thing Gary did take that medal, after all.'

'Yes,' said Fliss. 'If he hadn't got hold of it before the robbers came back, there'd have been no clue.'

'And if Gary had handed that medal in straightaway, they may well have been caught by now,' said Mrs Tenneson.

Gary blushed, and the others were silent. They could not deny this was true.

'What you all did was wrong,' said Mr Tenneson, 'and there's no getting away from it. You're simply lucky that things seem to have turned out so well.'

'Yes, Dad,' said Fliss.

'I'll have that key now, Zeke.' Mr Tenneson held out his hand.

Zeke took the key to the hut out of his pocket and fingered it lovingly. 'Can we go in, just for one last time?' he asked sadly.

Mr Tenneson looked at his wife, who nodded slightly.

'I don't see any harm in that,' she said. 'But after today, that hut stays locked until the Christmas holidays. Then we'll think about whether you can be trusted to have it back.'

'Thanks,' said Zeke.

Lisa felt sorry for Zeke. Losing the hut would be harder for him than for anyone, even Fliss.

The Gang sat down in their usual places without the customary chatter. Everyone seemed to sense that this was the last proper meeting they would have, anywhere. Lisa felt it in the silence, saw it in the solemn faces turned towards her. It was not just because of the hut. Things would never be the same again, and this time would be remembered, a little shame-facedly perhaps, as the summer when they stopped being really children. They would all be friends, for ever, but the Gang was gone. Old Fogarty and his apple trees could rest easy.

After a moment's silence, as though in memory of the old days that had passed, Zeke spoke. 'I think we need a last round-up of explanations,' he said. 'Fliss and I should start, since we were not around when we were needed. I'm sorry about that, Gary.'

Gary smiled, and shrugged his shoulders. Fliss and Zeke then explained that they had tried to get to the woods during the storm as well, but their mother had caught them just as they reached the back door.

'We told her we wanted to have a game in the hut during the storm,' said Fliss. 'You know, castaways and all that.'

'She told us not to be idiots and took the door key away,' said Zeke. 'They would have heard us going out the front way, so there was nothing we could do.'

'You were really brave, Lisa,' added Gary. 'I know how scared you are of the dark. I won't forget it.'

Shyly, he took her hand, and Lisa smiled gratefully.

'Your mum's great, too,' said Gary. 'I won't have to worry about Uncle Jack any more.'

'Why?' asked Lisa. 'What's happened?'

'Don't you know?'

'Know what?' Lisa looked at Fliss and Zeke. Their faces were as blank as her own. They all turned to Gary.

'Your mum's found somewhere for us to live,' he said. 'At least for a while, on a sort of trial basis, your mum calls it. Some Day Centre on the other side of Plymouth that your mum knows needs a new caretaker. The old one's retiring at the end of the month. Your mum recommended my mum for the job, and persuaded them to give her a try.'

'But how will your mum manage?' asked Lisa. 'I mean, how will she get to work?'

'No problem,' said Gary. 'The job's a live-in one, and the flat's on top of the centre. She won't have to travel at all. I think it will be hard for her, especially at first, because she's not used to people any more. But at least we'll be on our own. And anyway, Mum's going to get treatment for her agoraphobia. Your dad's convinced her it can be cured, and she promised me she'd give it a go.'

'Can it be cured?' asked Fliss.

Gary shrugged. 'I don't know. But he's certainly made my mum believe it.'

'Gary, what about your Uncle Jack?' Lisa really wanted to ask whether the hospital had found out where his bruises came from, but she didn't know how to do that tactfully.

Gary squeezed her hand; he understood. 'There was a really nice nurse at the hospital,' he said. 'She talked to me for ages. They knew someone had thumped me;

104

it wasn't as hard as I thought it would be to tell the truth. No one made me feel bad, they were just really kind and understood exactly how I felt. I don't know if anything will happen to Uncle Jack, but anyway he's been warned not to lay a finger on me again.'

There was a knock at the door. 'Can I come in?' It was Mr McBride. Zeke opened the door and he came in, stooping through the doorway. He looked very big in the small hut.

'What's happened? Any news?' They were all talking at once, and McBride raised his hand for silence with an amused smile.

'May I sit down?'

Fliss brought the bathroom stool and Mr McBride sat down facing them.

'We are pretty sure the car Mr Fogarty saw was used in the robbery,' he said. 'We think they went across the school field on foot, because a strange car outside Thurlow Park would be bound to cause comment, especially since there is a security guard patrolling the area at night. The thieves had reckoned without our Mr Fogarty's natural curiosity.'

Zeke laughed. 'I bet he'll be impossible now,' he said. 'He'll be telling everyone about how he captured dangerous robbers single-handed, and he'll never leave the window!'

'I expect you're right,' Mr McBride smiled. 'Anyway, they carried the stuff from the robbery across the school field and loaded it into the car, bold as brass. They thought they were being very clever, of course – we couldn't find any trace of a car, you see. But now we've got all our people on the lookout. Mr Fogarty did not take the number, but he can give a pretty good description of the car and the men inside. It won't be long before we have them; we already have an idea about who's responsible.'

'Wow!' said Gary. 'It's better than the television. You were brilliant, piecing the information together like that. I wouldn't mind being a policeman, one day,' he added awkwardly. 'If I grow tall enough, of course.'

McBride patted his shoulder and stood up to leave. 'I'm sure you will, son. Now I've got to get into work, so I can be there when the suspects are brought in. I have a feeling it won't be too long a wait. Goodbye.'

' 'Bye' they chorused.

Zeke's eyes were shining. 'Here, do you think they'll catch them today?'

'If my Dad says so, then they will,' said Lisa firmly. She leaned back on her cushion. For the first time in ages she felt happy; properly, full-of-smiles happy. And also, for the first time in ages that she could remember, Lisa was proud to be Detective Inspector George McBride's only daughter.

Other great reads ✦ *from* **Red Fox**

Further Red Fox titles that you might enjoy reading are listed on the following pages. They are available in bookshops or they can be ordered directly from us.

   If you would like to order books, please send this form and the money due to:

ARROW BOOKS, BOOKSERVICE BY POST, PO BOX 29, DOUGLAS, ISLE OF MAN, BRITISH ISLES. Please enclose a cheque or postal order made out to Arrow Books Ltd for the amount due, plus 22p per book for postage and packing, both for orders within the UK and for overseas orders.

NAME _____

ADDRESS _____

_____

Please print clearly.

Whilst every effort is made to keep prices low, it is sometimes necessary to increase cover prices at short notice. If you are ordering books by post, to save delay it is advisable to phone to confirm the correct price. The number to ring is THE SALES DEPARTMENT 071 (if outside London) 973 9700.

Other great reads from **Red Fox**

THE SNIFF STORIES Ian Whybrow

Things just keep happening to Ben Moore. It's dead hard
avoiding disaster when you've got to keep your street cred with
your mates *and* cope with a family of oddballs at the same time.
There's his appalling 2½ year old sister, his scatty parents who
are into healthy eating and animal rights and, worse than all
of these, there's Sniff! If only Ben could just get on with his
scientific experiments and his attempt at a world beating
Swampbeast score . . . but there's no chance of that while chaos
is just around the corner.

ISBN 0 09 9750406 £2.50

J.B. SUPERSLEUTH Joan Davenport

James Bond is a small thirteen-year-old with spots and
spectacles. But with a name like that, how can he help being
a supersleuth?

It all started when James and 'Polly' (Paul) Perkins spotted
a teacher's stolen car. After that, more and more mysteries
needed solving. With the case of the Arabian prince, the
Murdered Model, the Bonfire Night Murder and the Lost
Umbrella, JB's reputation at Moorside Comprehensive soars.

But some of the cases aren't quite what they seem . . .

ISBN 0 09 9717808 £1.99

Other great reads from **Red Fox**

The Maggie Series   Joan Lingard

MAGGIE 1: THE CLEARANCE

Sixteen-year-old Maggie McKinley's dreading the prospect of a whole summer with her granny in a remote Scottish glen. But the holiday begins to look more exciting when Maggie meets the Frasers. She soon becomes best friends with James and spends almost all her time with him. Which leads, indirectly, to a terrible accident . . .

ISBN 0 09 947730 0   £1.99

MAGGIE 2: THE RESETTLING

Maggie McKinley's family has been forced to move to a high rise flat and her mother is on the verge of a nervous breakdown. As her family begins to rely more heavily on her, Maggie finds less and less time for her schoolwork and her boyfriend James. The pressures mount and Maggie slowly realizes that she alone must control the direction of her life.

ISBN 0 09 949220 2   £1.99

MAGGIE 3: THE PILGRIMAGE

Maggie is now seventeen. Though a Glaswegian through and through, she is very much looking forward to a cycling holiday with her boyfriend James. But James begins to annoy Maggie and tensions mount. Then they meet two Canadian boys and Maggie finds she is strongly attracted to one of them.

ISBN 0 09 951190 8   £2.50

MAGGIE 4: THE REUNION

At eighteen, Maggie McKinley has been accepted for university and is preparing to face the world. On her first trip abroad, she flies to Canada to a summer au pair job and a reunion with Phil, the Canadian student she met the previous summer. But as usual in Maggie's life, events don't go quite as planned . . .

ISBN 0 09 951260 2   £2.50

Other great reads from **Red Fox**

Discover the wide range of exciting activity books from Red Fox

THE PAINT AND PRINT FUN BOOK
Steve and Megumi Biddle

Would you like to make a glittering bird? A colourful tiger? A stained-glass window? Or an old treasure map? Well, all you need are ordinary materials like vegetables, tinfoil, paper doilies, even your own fingers to make all kinds of amazing things—without too much mess.

Follow Steve and Megumi's step-by-step instructions and clear diagrams and you can make all kinds of professional designs—to hang on your wall or give to your friends.

ISBN 0 09 9644606   £2.50

CRAZY KITES   Peter Eldin

This book is a terrific introduction to the art of flying kites. There are lots of easy-to-assemble, different kites to make, from the basic flat kite to the Chinese dragon and the book also gives you clear instructions on launching, flying and landing. Kite flying is fun. Help yourself to a soaring good time.

ISBN 0 09 964550 5   £2.50

Other great reads ➛ from **Red Fox**

CRAZY PAINTING   Juliet Bawden

There are loads of imaginative ideas and suggstions in this easy-to-follow activity book all about painting. First it teaches you the basics: how to make your own vegetable dyes, mix paints, create a fabulous marbled effect and decorate ceramics. Then the fun begins. You can design your own curtains, make zany brooches for your friends, create your own colourful wrapping paper and amaze your family with hours of painting pleasure.

ISBN 0 09 954320 6   £2.25

DRESSING UP FUN   Terry Burrows

Dressing up is always fun—for a party, a play or just for a laugh! In Dressing Up Fun you'll find loads of ideas for all kinds of costumes and make-up. So whether you'd like to be a cowboy, punk or witch, superman, a princess or the Empire State Building, youll find them all in this book.

ISBN 0 09 965110 6   £2.99

Other great reads from **Red Fox**

AMAZING ORIGAMI FOR CHILDREN
Steve and Megumi Biddle

Origami is an exciting and easy way to make toys, decorations and all kinds of useful things from folded paper.

Use leftover gift paper to make a party hat and a fancy box. Or create a colourful lorry, a pretty rose and a zoo full of origami animals. There are over 50 fun projects in Amazing Origami.

Following Steve and Megumi's step-by-step instructions and clear drawings, you'll amaze your friends and family with your magical paper creations.

ISBN 0 09 9661802   £4.99

MAGICAL STRING   Steve and Megumi Biddle

With only a loop of string you can make all kinds of shapes, puzzles and games. Steve and Megumi Biddle provide all the instructions and diagrams that are needed to create their amazing string magic in another of their inventive and absorbing books.

ISBN 0 09 964470 3   £2.50